Dear Reader,

Looking back over the years, I find it hard to realize that twenty-six of them have gone by since I wrote my first book—*Sister Peters in Amsterdam*. It wasn't until I started writing about her that I found that once I had started writing, nothing was going to make me stop—and at that time I had no intention of sending the manuscript to a publisher. It was my daughter who urged me to try my luck.

I shall never forget the thrill of having my first book accepted. And it's still a thrill each time a new story is accepted. Writing is such a pleasure to me, and seeing a story unfolding on my old typewriter is like watching a film and wondering how it will end. Happily, of course.

To have so many of my books republished is such a delightful thing to happen, and I can only hope that those who read them will share my pleasure in seeing them on the bookshelves again...and will enjoy reading them.

Betty Neels

Betty Neels spent her childhood and youth in Devonshire before training as a nurse and midwife. She was an army nursing sister during the war, married a Dutchman and subsequently lived in Holland for fourteen years. She now lives with her husband in Dorset and has a daughter and grandson. Her hobbies are reading, animals, old buildings and, of course, writing. Betty started to write upon retirement from nursing, incited by a lady in a library bemoaning the lack of romantic novels. She has since become one of Harlequin's most prolific and well-loved authors.

THE BEST *of*

BETTY NEELS

A SMALL SLICE OF SUMMER

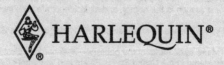

TORONTO • NEW YORK • LONDON
AMSTERDAM • PARIS • SYDNEY • HAMBURG
STOCKHOLM • ATHENS • TOKYO • MILAN • MADRID
PRAGUE • WARSAW • BUDAPEST • AUCKLAND

ISBN 0-373-51132-9

A SMALL SLICE OF SUMMER

First North American Publication 2001

This edition published by arrangement with Harlequin Books S.A.

® and TM are trademarks of the publisher. Trademarks indicated with ® are registered in the United States Patent and Trademark Office, the Canadian Trade Marks Office and in other countries.

Visit us at www.eHarlequin.com

Printed in U.S.A.

CHAPTER ONE

BIG BEN struck midday, and the sound, though muffled by the roar of London's traffic, struck clearly enough on Letitia Marsden's ear, causing her to put down the recovery tray she had been checking and look expectantly towards the doors separating theatre from the recovery room. Mr Snell had begun a Commando operation some three hours earlier; at any moment now the patient would be handed over to her care. The doors swung silently open at that very moment and she pressed the buzzer which would let the orderly know that she must come at once, and advanced to meet the theatre party and receive the still figure on the trolley from the hands of the scrub nurse.

'Hi, Tishy,' said that young lady in a cheerful whisper. 'Everything's OK, buzz if you want any help.' They cast a combined professional eye over the unconscious man between them. 'He's been a nasty colour once or twice, so keep your weather eye open.'

Letitia nodded. 'What's next? A cholecystectomy, isn't it?'

Her friend and colleague nodded. 'Yes—this one

5

should be fit to move before Sir gets through with it, though. The anaesthetist will be out presently—he's new by the way, filling in for Doctor van den Berg Effert.' She raised her brows in an exaggerated arch. 'Super, too.' she handed over the theatre slip, cast an eye on the clock, murmured: 'So long,' and slid back through the doors.

Letitia began her work, silent save for the muttered word now and then to the attendant orderly, one Mrs Mead, a middle-aged lady of great good sense, who had the added virtue of doing exactly what she was asked to do without arguing about it—her whole mind, save for one minute portion of it, concentrated upon her task, and that tiny portion concealed so deliberately beneath her calm cringed away from the grotesque appearance of the patient; the flap of skin already grafted, later to be used to cover the extensive operation on his throat, gave the man, lying so still, a quite unhuman appearance, and yet she was fully aware that later, given skilled nursing, expert skin grafting and time, his appearance could be made perfectly acceptable even to the most sensitive. She noted his pulse, his pupil reactions and his breathing, charted her findings, and because his colour wasn't quite to her satisfaction, turned on the oxygen. She was adjusting it when the door opened and a gowned and masked figure came unhurriedly in, to join her at the patient's side. A large man, very tall, and when he pulled down his mask, extremely handsome with it, with fair hair already flecked with grey, bright blue eyes and a long straight nose whose winged nostrils gave him a somewhat arrogant expression. But his mouth was kind when he smiled, and he was smiling at her now. She didn't smile back; since her unfortunate experience with the Medical Registrar she distrusted men—that was to say, all men under the age of fifty or so. She frowned at him, her eyes beneath their dark brows as bright a blue as his, her ordinary face, with its run-of-the-mill nose and large generous mouth, framed by the theatre mob cap which concealed the great quantity of dark brown hair she wore in a well-ordered coil on the top of her head.

'OK?' asked the giant mildly.

She handed him the chart with its quarter-hourly observations. 'His colour isn't quite as good as it was,' she stated, 'I've started the oxygen.'

He nodded and handed back the chart, looking at her now, instead of the patient. 'Call me if you want me,' he answered her, still very mild. 'The name's Mourik van Nie.' He turned on his heel and slid through the doors, making no sound, and moving, considering his size, very fast.

She got on with her work, saying what was necessary to Mrs Mead, her mind on her patient. It was only after an hour, when the giant had been back

once more, pronounced the patient fit to be transferred to the Intensive Care Unit and gone again,
that she allowed herself to speculate who he was.
Dutch, she supposed, like Doctor van den Berg Effert, one of the few men she liked and trusted and
wasn't shy of; but then he was married to Georgina,
her elder sister's close friend; they had trained together and now Margo was Sister on the Children's
Unit, and Georgina lived in the lap of luxury and a
state of married bliss in Doctor van den Berg Effert's lovely home in Essex. She and Margo had
been there to stay once or twice and Letitia, living
in a fool's paradise in which the Medical Registrar
was the only important being, had imagined herself
living like that too—only it hadn't turned out like
that at all; he had taken her out for a month or two,
talking vaguely about a future, which she, in her
besotted state, had already imagined into a fact
which wasn't fact at all, only daydreams, and then,
when she had refused to go away with him for the
weekend, had turned the daydream into a nightmare
with a jibing speech about old-fashioned girls who
should move with the times, and ending with the
remark that she wasn't even pretty... She had
known that, of course, but she had always thought
that when one fell in love, looks didn't matter so
very much, but she had been too hurt to say anything, and how did one begin to explain that being

the middle girl in a family of five daughters, strictly but kindly brought up by a mother with decidedly old-fashioned ideas and a father who was rector of a small parish in the depths of rural Devon was hardly conducive to being the life and soul of the swinging set.

She had said nothing at all, not because she was a meek girl, but because she was too choked with hurt pride and rage to make sense. She had thought of several telling speeches to make since that unhappy occasion, but since he worked on the Medical Wing and she spent her days in Theatre Unit, there was small chance of their meeting—and a good thing too, although her friends, meaning it kindly, kept her informed of his movements. He was currently wrapped up with Jean Mitchell, the blonde staff nurse on Orthopaedics, whom no one liked anyway; Letitia, in her more peevish moments, wished them well of each other.

The Commando case was transferred to the ICU.; she handed him over to the Sister-in-charge, repeated the instructions she had been given, put his charts into her superior's hands, and raced back to the recovery room. The cholecystectomy would be out at any moment now and she had to fetch the fresh recovery tray and see that Mrs Mead had cleared the other one away and tidied up. They were nicely ready when the doors swung silently open once more. It had been a straightforward case; she received her instructions, obeyed them implicitly, and when the anaesthetist loomed silently beside her, handed him the chart without speaking; there was no need to tell him the things he could see for himself: the patient was ready to go to the ward and she stood quietly waiting for him to tell her so, which he did with an unhurried: 'OK, Staff, wheel her away. There's an end-to-end coming out in a few minutes, old and frail; do what you can and let me know if you need me.'

And so the day wore on. Letitia was relieved for a late dinner and found the canteen almost empty, though the Main Theatre staff nurse was still there and a handful of nurses who had been delayed by various emergencies.

Letitia wandered along the counter with her tray, looking for something cheap and nourishing; she had bought a dress on her last days off and her pocket was now so light that buying her meals had become a major exercise in basic arithmetic. She chose soup, although it was a warm June day, a roll to go with it and a slab of treacle tart, because starch was filling and even though it was fattening too she was lucky enough not to have that problem, being possessed of a neat little figure which retained its slender curves whatever she ate. She paid for these dainties at the end of the counter and went to join her fellow staff nurse, Angela Collins, who cast a sympathetic eye at the contents of her tray, said fervently: 'Thank God it's only a week to pay-day,' and addressed herself to her own, similar meal.

Letitia nodded. 'Holidays in four weeks,' she observed cheerfully, and thought with sudden longing of the quiet Rectory. The raspberries would be ripe, she would go into the garden and walk up and down the canes, eating as many as she wanted. She sighed and asked: 'How's theatre? There's only that resection left, isn't there?'

Her friend snorted. 'There was—they popped two more on the list while Sister wasn't looking. She's fighting mad, but Mr Snell's doing his famous wheedling act and that new man has the charm turned full on—he's got her all girlish. I must say he's rather a dream; a pity he's only here while our Julius takes a holiday.'

'I thought you liked him.'

'Our Julius? Of course I do—we all dote on him, but he's married, isn't he? To your sister's best friend, too.'

Letitia nibbled at her roll, making it last. 'Yes, she's a sweetie, too.'

She wolfed down the treacle tart. 'I've still got some tea, shall we make a pot?'

They hurried over to the Nurses' Home and climbed to the top floor where the staff nurses had their rooms, and because there were several girls off duty, the tea was stretched to half a dozen mugs, sipped in comfort on Letitia's bed to the accompaniment of a buzz of conversation until she looked at her watch, discovered that she was almost late, and flew back through the hospital once more, walking sedately in those parts where she was likely to meet Authority, who frowned on running nurses, and tearing like mad along the long empty back corridors.

The afternoon went fast; it was half past four before the last case was wheeled away to the ward and Letitia, aided by the faithful Mrs Mead, began clearing up. Between them they had the place stripped, cleaned and put together again by the time Big Ben chimed five o'clock. Mrs Mead had gone and Letitia had taken off her theatre dress and mob cap and was standing in the middle of the room doing absolutely nothing when the giant walked in once more.

'Not got home yet?' he asked carelessly as he crossed to the outside door. 'Good afternoon to you.' He smiled vaguely in her direction and she heard him walking rapidly along the corridor which led to the wards. When she couldn't hear his footsteps any more she took one final look round the recovery room and went in her turn out of the door. As she passed the Surgical Wing she caught a glimpse of him, standing outside Sister's office, deep in conversation with Staff Nurse Bolt, another friend of

hers. They were both laughing and it made her feel
a little lonely: he could have stopped and talked to
her, too.

She had to hear of him later that evening, when
half a dozen of them were sitting round consuming
the chips they had been down the road to buy—
cheaper than the canteen and filling—besides, someone had come back from days off with a large fruit
cake and, between them they had gathered tea and
sugar and milk and made a giant pot of tea. They
had cast off their frilly caps and their shoes and
some of them were already in dressing gowns and
the noise was considerable. It was Angela who
brought up the subject of the newcomer. 'He's fab,'
she uttered to anyone who cared to listen, 'huge and
smashing to look at, and one of those lovely slow,
deep voices.' She turned her head to look for Letitia,
pouring tea. 'Hey, Tishy, you must have had time
to take a good look—didn't you think he was absolutely super? Just about the most super man
you've ever set eyes on?'

There was silence for a few seconds; every girl
in the room knew about Tishy and the Medical Registrar, and because they all liked her they had done
their best to help her by saying nothing about it and
ignoring her pinched face and red eyes. It was a pity
that Angela hadn't stopped to think. Several of them
spoke at once to save Tishy from answering, but she

spoke with her usual composure. 'I didn't really look at him—we were too busy. He knows his job, though.'

There was a chorus of relieved agreement before someone wanted to know if the rest of them had seen the trouser suits in Peter Robinson's, and the talk turned, as it so often did, to clothes.

Letitia was on duty at eight o'clock the next morning. The list was heavy enough to begin with, petering out after dinner time, so that by four o'clock she was clearing the recovery room in the pleasant anticipation of getting off duty punctually at half past four. As indeed she was. She wandered through the hospital on the way to her room; several of her friends were off duty too, they might have a few sets of tennis, it was a lovely day still. She stopped to look out of a window and saw Doctor Mourik van Nie getting into a car—a splendid BMW convertible. She studied its sleek lines and admired the discreet grey of its coachwork before she turned away, wondering where he was going.

Jason Mourik van Nie was going to Dalmers Place. An hour or so later he joined Julius van den Berg Effert and Georgina on the terrace behind the house. Polly, their very small daughter, was almost asleep on her father's knee and Georgina exclaimed in relief as he walked out of the french windows. 'There you are—Polly refuses to go to bed until you've kissed her good night.' She smiled at her husband's friend. 'If you'll do that right away. I'll whisk her off to bed and Julius shall get us all a drink.'

Jason smiled at her, kissed his small goddaughter, exchanged a brief '*Dag*' and sat down.

'Stay where you are, darling,' said Julius, 'I'll pop this young woman into her bed and bring the drinks as I come back.'

His wife gave him a warm smile. 'Tell Nanny I'll be up in ten minutes unless Ivo starts to cry.' Her smile widened and Julius grinned back at her; Ivo was just two months old, a tiny replica of his father, whereas little Polly was like her mother with a gentle prettiness and most of her charm. She wound a small arm round her father's neck now and smiled sleepily at him as he carried her into the house.

Jason watched them go. 'Julius is a lucky man,' he said quietly. 'You, and the enchanting Polly, and now Ivo.'

'I'm lucky too,' Georgina told him, 'I've got Julius.'

'I hope someone says that about me one day,' he observed. 'May I smoke my pipe?'

She nodded. 'Of course. Did you have a busy day?'

'So-so. One Commando to start with and a couple of abdominals, then we petered out with appendices.

Snell was operating again. Oh—Theatre Sister sent her love, I've forgotten what she said her name was and I couldn't identify her very well; she was gowned up and masked, the only face I've seen clearly in these last few days was in the recovery room—quite unremarkable, though—it belongs to someone called Tishy.'

Georgina smiled. 'Little Tishy. She's Margo's young sister—she must be twenty-three, I suppose, she qualified six months ago. You didn't like her?'

Jason stretched his long legs and studied his enormous, beautifully shod feet. 'I hadn't really thought about it,' he admitted carelessly. 'Mousey girls with heavy frowns aren't quite my line.'

'Oh, she doesn't frown all the time,' stated Georgina quickly, 'it's only because you're a man,' and as her companion's brows shot up: 'She was almost engaged to the Medical Registrar, but he switched his interest to a dashing blonde on Orthopaedics—I daresay she was more accommodating. I don't know what he said to poor little Tishy, but ever since then she's shied away from anything male under fifty.'

'Julius too?'

'Julius is thirty-seven,' his loving wife reminded him, 'but Margo is a friend of mine and of course I know Tishy too; she's been here once or twice, so she knows Julius quite well as well as working for him. He takes care to be casually friendly, bless him. She's a splendid nurse.'

She turned her head and her eyes lighted up as they always did when she saw her husband.

'Sorry I was so long,' he apologized as he set the tray of drinks down. 'Great-Uncle Ivo telephoned—wants to know when we're going over to Bergenstijn. I told him we'd be there before the summer's over. The theatre's closing at the end of July, we'll go then if you would like that, my love.'

Georgina agreed happily. 'Lovely, Julius—we can all go. Cor and Beatrix and Franz-Karel can drive them over. Dimphena will be with Jan, I suppose, but they could come over...'

Jason studied his glass. 'What a quiverful you took on when you married Julius,' he observed idly, 'four cousins of assorted ages.'

'Don't forget Polly and Ivo. But the others—they're not small any more; Karel's a post-graduate and almost finished with hospital, and Franz is sixteen, that only leaves Beatrix and Cor, and now Dimphena is married there's quite a gap.'

'Which we shall doubtless fill within the next few years,' commented her husband softly.

'I'm envious,' said Jason slowly, and Georgina threw him a quick glance.

'No need,' she told him kindly, 'you only have to

lift a finger for all the prettiest girls to come running.'

'That's all very well as well as being grossly exaggerated, but none of these same girls had ever succeeded in convincing me that I can't live without her.'

Georgina got up. 'One day there'll be a girl,' she assured him, 'though probably she won't be pretty or come running. I'm going to see to Ivo.'

She ran indoors and the two men sat in silence for a few minutes, Presently Jason spoke. 'As I said to Georgina just now, you're a lucky devil, Julius.'

'Yes, I know.' He added thoughtfully, 'I was thirty-three when I first met Georgina.'

'A reminder that I'm thirty-five and still haven't met my paragon?' They both laughed before plunging into a discussion as to how the day had gone in theatre, absorbed in their world of anaesthetics.

It was later that evening as Georgina sat before her dressing table brushing her hair that she said suddenly: 'Julius, can you think of a good reason for having Tishy down here?'

Her husband's eyes met hers in the mirror. 'Tishy?' he queried mildly. 'Why Tishy, darling?'

'She could be exhausted,' went on Georgina, taking no notice, 'worn out with work and needing a few days' rest...'

Julius had become adept at reading his wife's mind. 'She would have to work fast.'

Georgina gave him a doubtful look. 'That won't do, then,' she stated positively. 'I daresay she can't bear the sight of him, and he's hardly noticed her.'

'My love, is it wise to play providence? They're a most unlikely pair; just because Tishy is getting over hurt pride and Jason chooses to remain a care-free bachelor it doesn't mean that they'll fall into each other's arms.'

'No, I can see that, but it would be nice. If we just gave them the chance…'

But as it turned out there was no need of that.

Two days later, with the list almost over for the day, Letitia was starting on the clearing up, her mind happily occupied with plans for her days off, due to start in the morning. Two days, she mused, and almost no money so she wouldn't be able to go home, but she could go to Epping, where an elderly aunt lived—no telephone, unfortunately, but Aunt Maud never minded an unexpected visitor for a couple of days. She had a dear little house on the edge of the forest and it would be pleasant after the heat and rush of London and the hospital. If Margo had been there they could have gone together, but she was on holiday, up in Scotland with friends. Letitia nodded her head in satisfaction, glad that she had made up her mind, and looked impatiently at the theatre doors; the case should have been finished by now, it was hernia and shouldn't have to stay long in her care. She looked at the clock, calculating how soon she could get away that evening, then turned round to see who it was who had just come in from the outer door.

It was the very last person she wanted to see; Mike Brent, the Medical Registrar, lounging in, very sure of himself, his good-looking face wearing a smile which not so very long ago would have melted her heart and now, rather to her surprise, made no impression upon it at all.

'Hullo,' he said, 'how's little Tishy? Haven't seen you around for quite a few weeks—I was beginning to think you might have run away.'

She eyed him steadily. 'Why should you think that?'

He shrugged his shoulders. 'Oh, well—no hard feelings.'

She arranged a recovery tray just so before she answered him. 'I'm busy, there's a case...'

He interrupted her impatiently. 'Oh, come off it, Tishy. To tell you the truth I've been a bit worried; didn't like to think of you feeling jilted and all that, you know—after all, I couldn't help it if you took me seriously, could I? And you're a bit out of date, aren't you. I mean, the odd weekend doesn't mean a thing...'

'It does to me.' Neither of them heard the theatre door open, Doctor Mourik van Nie's voice startled them both. 'Perhaps if I might break into this most interesting discussion on your love life?' he suggested placidly, and turned to Letitia to study her furious face with gentle amusement.

'This next case coming in within a few minutes—she's not so good.' He ignored the other man completely and began to give her instructions; by the time he had finished Mike had gone.

She boiled with temper while she dealt competently with her patient, damping down her furious thoughts so that she might concentrate on the matter in hand. Only some half an hour later, the patient transferred to the ward, nicely on the road to recovery again, did she allow her mind to dwell on the unfortunate episode which had occurred. And funnily enough it was the Dutchman she was furious with; for coming in like that and overhearing Mike talking all that hot air. She paused, aware that his words, which at one time would have been quite shattering to her, were, in fact, just that. She had, let her face it, been a fool; she was well rid of him, even if her pride was still ragged at the edges. But that Doctor Mourik van Nie should have been a witness to such a nasty little scene—that was a different matter entirely; he must have found it amusing; he had stared at her as though he had never seen her before. She felt unreasonably annoyed about that, so that she clashed and banged her way around the recovery room before finally leaving it in a state of perfection. The quicker she got out of the hospital and into Aunt Maud's placid company, the better.

In her room she flung a few things into an overnight bag, changed into the tan jersey cardigan suit with the shell pink blouse she had bought instead of eating properly that month, coiled her long hair neatly on the top of her head and, nicely made up, dashed out to catch a bus.

The Underground was crowded; she didn't get a seat until the train had left Leytonstone, and it was a relief when she at last got out at Epping and went into the street. The crowds were a little less now, but the rush hour wasn't quite over; track was still heavy coming from London. She was standing on the kerb waiting to cross the street when a group of people passing her unthinkingly shoved her off the curb into the path of the oncoming cars. She had a momentary glimpse of a sleek grey bonnet and heard the squeal of brakes as the bumper tipped her off balance. She fell, hoping desperately that her new out fit wouldn't be ruined, aware as she fell that she had done so awkwardly and that her left ankle hurt most abominably. She had no chance to think after that, because Doctor Mourik van Nie was bending over her. 'Well, I'm damned,' he said, and then: 'Does anything hurt? The bumper caught you and you fell awkwardly.'

Letitia sat up, glad of his arm, comfortably firm, round her shoulders. 'I was trying to save my dress. It's my ankle, otherwise I'm fine.'

A small crowd had collected, but the doctor took no notice of it, merely scooped her neatly off the ground and carried her to the car, where he sat her carefully on the front seat. 'Let's have a look,' he suggested calmly, and slid her sandal off a decidedly swollen ankle. 'A sprain, I fancy. Stockings or tights?'

'Tights.'

He produced a pair of scissors from a pocket. 'Sorry about this—I'll get you another pair,' he promised as he made a neat slit and cut the nylon neatly way above the ankle. He was reaching for his bag in the back of the car when the policeman arrived. Letitia sat back, listening to the doctor's quiet answers to the officer's questions, the eager chorus of witnesses, anxious to allow no blame to rest upon him, and her own voice, a little wobbly, giving her name and address and where she was going and why. By the time things had been sorted out the ankle had been firmly bandaged and her head was beginning to ache. She didn't listen to what the doctor said to the policeman—indeed, she barely noticed when he got in beside her and started the car;

she was suddenly sleepy. The car was comfortable to the point of luxury; she closed her eyes.

They were almost at Dalmers Place when she woke up again; she recognized the road almost at once. 'I was going to my aunt in Epping,' she began worriedly. 'My days off, you know.'

'You went to sleep—the best thing for you. Does she expect you?'

'No.'

'Then there's nothing to worry about. I'm taking you to Dalmers Place. You're a friend of Georgina, aren't you—and Julius? They'll be delighted to put you up for the night.'

She turned to look at him, quite shocked. 'Oh, you can't do that—invite me there without them knowing, whatever will they say? If you'd stop... oh, dear, we've gone through Bishop's Stortford, haven't we? Could you go a little out of your way to Saffron Walden? There's a station there—I could get on a train back to Epping.'

'Hopping all the way? Don't be absurd. Besides, I feel responsible for you—I knocked you down.'

'But it wasn't your fault, and really I can't allow you...'

He interrupted her in a placid voice. 'Dear girl, what a mountain you are making out of this little molehill! And you know that you're dying to get to bed and nurse that painful ankle.'

She had to laugh a little then and he gave her a quick sideways glance and said: 'That's better,' and a moment later slowed the car to allow Mr Legg, who did the garden and lived in the lodge at Dalmers Place, to come out and open the gate for them, and then drove, still slowly, up the short, tree-lined drive to the house where he stopped before its door, told her to stay where she was, got out, and went round the side of the house.

Georgina looked up as he reached the terrace. 'Hullo,' she greeted him cheerfully. 'We were just beginning to wonder what had happened to you.'

'I've brought someone with me, I hope you won't mind—it's Tishy.'

He was quick to see the quick look his friends exchanged and went on smoothly, 'I could take her on...' to be cut short by Georgina's fervent: 'No, Jason—we're delighted, really, only Julius and I were talking about her—oh, quite casually,' she avoided her husband's twinkling eye, 'and it's funny, isn't it, how when you talk about someone they often turn up unexpectedly. Where have you left her?'

'In the car. She sprained her ankle—I knocked her down.'

Georgina was already leading the way. 'Oh, how unfortunate!' she exclaimed, meaning exactly the opposite. She glanced at Julius over her shoulder and when Jason wasn't looking, pulled a face at him. 'But we must thank Providence that it was you, if you see what I mean.'

CHAPTER TWO

LETITIA SAT in the car, feeling a fool. Her ankle throbbed, so did her head, and she had been pitch-forked into a situation which had been none of her doing. Probably Georgina would be furious at hav-ing an unexpected guest at less than a moment's notice. True, she had been to Dalmers Place before, but only in the company of her sister Margo—it was Margo who was Georgina's friend. She sought fe-verishly for a solution to her problem and came up with nothing practical, and when the three of them came round the house and crossed the grass towards the car, she found herself studying their faces for signs of annoyance. She could see none; Georgina was looking absolutely delighted and her husband was smiling, and as for Doctor Mourik van Nie, he wore the pleased look of one who had done his duty and could now wash his hands of the whole tiresome affair.

Georgina reached the car first. 'Tishy,' she ex-claimed, 'you poor girl—does it hurt very much? You shall go straight to bed and the men shall take another look at it—you look as though you could do with a drink, too. Thank heaven it was Jason who

knocked you down and not some stranger who
wouldn't have known what to do.' She paused for
breath and Letitia said quickly: 'I'm awfully sorry—
I mean, coming suddenly like this and being so awkward.' Her eyes searched Georgina's face anxiously.
'You don't mind?'

'Of course not, it'll be fun once that ankle stops
aching.' She stood aside while Julius said Hullo in
a welcoming way and Jason said matter-of-factly:
'I'll carry you in.'

'I can hobble, I'm sure I can.'

He grinned. 'I shouldn't bet on that if I were you.'
He had opened the car door and swept her carefully
into his arms. 'Which room?' he asked Georgina.

'Turn left at the top of the stairs, down the little
passage, the second door.'

Letitia wondered if the doctor found her heavy;
apparently not, for he climbed the staircase at a good
pace and with no huffing or puffing, found her room
without difficulty and sat her down in a chair. 'Georgina will help you undress,' he told her with impersonal kindness, 'and we'll come back later and take
another look at the ankle.' He had gone before she
could frame her thanks.

Half an hour later she was sitting up in bed, nicely
supported by pillows and with the bedclothes turned
back to expose her foot; by now the ankle was badly
swollen and discoloured. The men came in together

with Georgina and Letitia wasn't sure whether to be pleased or not when neither gave her more than a cursory glance before bending over the offending joint, which they agreed was nothing more than a partial tear of the ligament and hardly justified an X-ray. 'We'll strap it,' they told her. 'You'll have to rest it for three or four days, then you can start active use—a couple of weeks and you'll be as good as new.'

'A couple of weeks? But I've only got two days off!' She was appalled at their verdict.

'Sick leave?' suggested Doctor Mourik van Nie. He sounded positively fatherly.

She stared at him; they were all being very kind, but she was spoiling their evening. She said quickly: 'If I could go back to St Athel's with you in the morning—there's a list at nine o'clock, isn't there?—I could see someone. That's if you wouldn't mind taking me.'

He gave her a long considered look and she felt her cheeks grow red.

'No, I won't take you, you silly girl. Georgina has already said that you're to stay here until Julius pronounces you fit to travel, and that won't be for a few days.'

'Of course you'll stay,' chimed in Georgina warmly. 'I shall love having you; these two are driv-ing up to Edinburgh at the weekend, to some meeting or other, and I wasn't looking forward to being alone one bit. And now I'm going to see about your dinner, you must be famished.'

'And I'll telephone St Athel's,' Julius suggested, and left the room with his wife, leaving Doctor Mourik van Nie lounging on the side of the bed.

'That's settled,' he commented, and smiled at her, and for some reason she remembered that he had smiled that afternoon when he had come upon her and Mike.

'You're all very kind,' she said crossly, because her head still ached, 'but I don't like being a nuisance.'

He got to his feet so that she had to tilt her head to look up at him.

'My dear girl,' he said, and his voice was bland, 'the sooner you stop imagining that because one man said you were—er—old-fashioned, the rest of us are villains and you're a failure, the better. I'm surprised at you; you seem to me to be a sensible enough girl, and when you smile you're quite pretty.'

He strolled to the door. 'You'll feel better in the morning,' he assured her as he went out.

Letitia stared at the shut door; probably she would feel much better in the morning, at the moment she felt quite sick with surprise and temper—how dared

he talk to her like that?—it was possibly these strong
feelings which caused her to burst into tears.

She was wiping her eyes when Georgina came
back, and she, after one quick glance, made some
thoughtful remark about delayed shock and proffered the glass of sherry she had brought with her.
'Dinner in half an hour,' she said cheerfully, 'and
Julius says a good night's sleep is a must, so he's
coming along with a sleeping pill later on.'

Letitia sipped the sherry. 'I've never taken one in
my life,' she protested, and then remembering what
the Dutchman had said, added meekly: 'But I will
if he says so.'

She felt a lot better after her dinner and better still
after a long night's sleep. Indeed, she woke early
and lay watching the sun gathering strength for another warm day, and she heard the car drive away
too. That would be Doctor Mourik van Nie, she supposed, and she felt an unreasonable pique because
he hadn't come to inquire how she felt, but of course
she wasn't his patient, only an unfortunate incident
at the end of a long day.

She sat up in bed, wincing a little at the pain in
her ankle, and thought about him, willing to admit,
now that it was morning and she was feeling better,
that he had been quite right even if a little outspoken, the previous evening. She had been sorry for
herself, she admitted that now, although she hadn't

much liked being dubbed as sensible, but he had said that she was almost pretty when she smiled. She smiled now, remembering it, and turned a beaming face upon the maid who presently tapped on the door with her early morning tea.

The day rolled along on well-oiled wheels; the house came alive, breakfasted, and settled down to the morning. Julius came early, examined the ankle, pronounced it to be going along nicely and left Georgina to help her out of bed and into a chair by the window and presently they all had their coffee there, with Polly playing happily and baby Ivo asleep in his cot. It was when Julius got up to go to his study that Letitia asked a little diffidently if he had telephoned the hospital.

'Did I forget to tell you? You are to stay here until I consider it all right for you to travel, and it has been left to me to decide if you need a week off after that.'

She was unaware of how plainly her thoughts showed on her face. 'Home for a few days?' suggested Georgina, reading them correctly. 'One of the men can take you up to town and drop you off at the station...' She stopped and smiled, looking so pleased with herself that Letitia was on the point of asking why, but Julius spoke first, to say that he would be back very shortly and carry her down to the garden. 'Far too nice a day to stay indoors,' he pointed out kindly, and when she thanked him, adding that she hoped she wasn't being a nuisance, he went on: 'Of course not—we're treating you as one of the family, Tishy, and Georgina's delighted to have your company while we're away, and in any case, just to prove how much we take you for granted, I'm driving her to Saffron Walden very shortly. Nanny will be here with the babies, of course, and Stephens will bring you your lunch and see that you're comfortable. You don't mind?'

He had struck the right note; she felt at ease now because she wasn't spoiling their day after all. 'Of course I don't mind—it will be super doing nothing. You're both so kind.'

Julius went away and Georgina smiled and offered to get a rather fetching housecoat of a pleasing shade of pink for her guest to wear. Letitia put it on, admiring the fine lawn and tucks and lace. It had a pie-frill collar and cuffed sleeves, and looking down at her person, she had to admit that lovely clothes did something for one...'I can leave my hair, can't I?' she asked. 'There's no one to see.'

Her kind hostess bent down to pick up a hairpin. She said: 'No one, Tishy,' hoping that Providence, already so kind, would continue to be so.

The day was glorious. Letitia, lying comfortably on a luxurious day bed, leafed through the pile of glossy magazines she had been provided with, ate a delicious lunch Mrs Stephens had arranged so temptingly on the trays Stephens carried out to her, then closed her eyes. It was warm in the sun; she would have a crop of freckles in no time, but it really didn't matter. She had spent a lot of money she really couldn't afford on a jar of something or other to prevent them, because Mike had told her once that he thought they were childish. Thinking about it now, she began to wonder exactly what it was about her that he had liked. Whatever it had been, it hadn't lasted long. She remembered with faint sickness how he had told her that she wasn't pretty. 'Not even pretty,' he had said, as though there was nothing else about her that was attractive. She frowned at the thought and pondered the interesting question as to what Doctor Mourik van Nie would find attractive in a girl. Whatever it was, she felt very sure that she hadn't got it. She dozed off, frowning a little.

She woke up half an hour later, much refreshed, and saw him sitting in an outside garden chair, his large hands locked behind his head, his eyes shut. She looked at him for a few seconds, wondering if he were really asleep and why was he there anyway; her watch told her that it was barely half past two; theatre should have gone on until at least four o'clock. Perhaps, she thought childishly, he wasn't really there; he had been the last person she had thought about before she went to sleep—he could be the tail end of a dream. She shut her eyes and opened them again and found him still there, looking at her now. 'You've got freckles,' he observed, and unlike Mike, he sounded as though he rather liked them.

'Yes, I know—I hate them. I bought some frightfully expensive cream to get rid of them, but it didn't work.'

'They're charming, let them be.' His voice was impersonal and casually friendly and she found herself smiling. 'I thought theatre was working until four o'clock today.'

'It was, but at half past twelve precisely some workman outside in the street pickaxed his way through the hospital's water supply. Luckily we were on the tail end of an op, but we had to pack things up for the day. Do you mind if I go to sleep?'

She felt absurdly offended. 'Not in the least,' she told him in an icy little voice, and picked up a magazine. Unfortunately it was *Elle* and her French not being above average, looking at it was a complete waste of time; even the prices of the various way-out garments displayed in its pages meant nothing to her, because she couldn't remember how many francs went to a pound.

'You're a very touchy girl,' observed her companion, his eyes shut, and while she was still trying to find a suitable retort to this remark:

'Am I right in suspecting that this—what's his name—the Medical Registrar was the first man you ever thought you were in love with?'

She sat up and swung her legs over the side of the daybed. 'I won't stay here!' she exploded. 'You have no right…you don't even know me…ouch!'

She had put her injured foot to the ground and it had hurt. The doctor got out of his chair in a patient kind of way, lifted the stricken limb back on to the daybed, said: 'Lie still, do—and don't be so bird-witted,' and went back to his chair. His voice was astringent, but his hands had been very gentle. 'And don't be so damned sensitive; I'm not a young man on the look out for a girl, you know. I'm thirty-five and very set in my ways—ask Julius.' He closed his eyes again. 'I'm ever so safe, like an uncle.' There was a little pause, then he opened one eye. 'I like that pink thing and your hair hanging loose.'

Letitia had listened to him in amazement and a kind of relief because now she could think of him as she thought of Julius; kind and friendly and big brotherish. Two short months ago, if Mike had said that, she would have been in a flutter, now it didn't register at all—at least, she admitted to herself, it was nice that he liked her hair. She took a quick peep and was disappointed to see that his eyes were closed once more.

He wasn't asleep, though. 'Where is your home?' he asked presently.

She cast *Elle* aside with relief. 'Devonshire, near Chagford—that's a small town on Dartmoor. Father's the rector of a village a few miles on to the moor.'

'Mother? Brothers and sisters?' His voice was casually inquiring.

'Mother and four sisters.'

His eyes flew open. 'Are they all like you?'

She wasn't sure how to take that, but she answered soberly: 'No, they're all pretty. Hester—she's the second eldest—is married, so's Miriam, she comes after me, and Paula's the last.'

'And where do you come?'

'In the middle.'

'And your eldest sister—Margo, isn't it? She's George's friend?'

'Yes, they trained together. Margo's away on holiday. She's going to get engaged any day now.'

He opened an eye. 'I always thought,' he stated seriously, 'that the young lady about to be proposed to was suitably surprised.'

Letitia giggled, and just for a few moments, in her pink gown and her shining curtain of hair, looked, even with the freckles peppering her nose, quite pretty, so that the doctor opened the other eye as well.

'She and Jack have known each other ever since she was fifteen, but he went abroad—he's a bridge engineer, so Margo has gone on working while he got his feet on the ladder, as it were, and now he's got a marvellous job and they can buy a house and get married.'

'And you will be a bridesmaid at the wedding, no doubt?'

'Well, no—you see, we drew lots and Miriam and Paula won. It's a bit expensive to have four brides-maids.'

The corners of his firm mouth twitched faintly. 'I daresay two are more than ample. I have often wondered why girls had them.'

She gazed at him earnestly as she explained: 'Well, they make everything look pretty—I mean, the bride wants to look nicer than anyone else, but bridesmaids make a background for her.'

'Ah, yes—stupid of me. Do you set great store on bridesmaids, Letitia?'

She was about to tell him that she hadn't even thought about it, but that would have been a colossal fib; when she had imagined herself to be in love with Mike, her head had been full of such things. 'I used to think it was frightfully important, but now I don't imagine it matters at all.'

'You know, I think you may be right.' He heaved himself out of the chair and stretched enormously. 'I'm going to get us a long cool drink and ask Stephens if we can have tea in half an hour. Can I do anything for you on my way?'

She shook her head and sat back, feeling the sun tracing more freckles and not caring. She wasn't sure what had happened, but she felt as though Jason Mourik van Nie had opened a door for her and she had escaped. It was a lovely feeling.

The drinks were long and iced and he had added straws to her glass. She supped the coolness with delight and exclaimed: 'Oh, isn't this just super?' then felt awkward because he might not find it super at all.

'Very.' He was lying back again, not looking at her. 'Do you suppose you could remember to call me Jason? I call you Tishy, you know, although on second thoughts I think I'll call you Letitia, I like it better.'

'Mother always calls me that, but they call me Tishy at the hospital, and sometimes my sisters do too when they want me to do something for them.'

They had their tea presently in complete harmony and she quite forgot to wonder where Georgina and Julius had got to, and when Nanny came out with Ivo in his pram and Polly got on to the doctor's knee, she lay back, listening to him entertaining the moppet with a series of rhymes in his own language, apparently quite comprehensible to her small ears. She watched him idly, thinking that it was pleasant doing nothing with someone you liked. She gave herself a mental shake; only a very short time ago she hadn't liked him, but when she tried to remember the exact moment when she had stopped disliking him and liking him instead, she was unable to do so. Her thoughts became a little tangled and she abandoned them when Jason broke in on her musings with the suggestion that she might like to recite a nursery rhyme or two and give him a rest. She had got through 'Hickory, Dickory, Dock' and was singing 'Three Blind Mice' in a high sweet, rather breathy voice when Georgina and Julius joined them and the little party became a cheerful gossiping group, with Ivo tucked in his mother's arms and Polly transferred to her father.

'Ungrateful brat,' remarked Jason pleasantly. 'Letitia and I are hoarse with our efforts to amuse her and now she has no eyes or ears for anyone but her papa.'

'You got back early?' Georgina asked, and smiled a little.

Jason repeated the tale of the workman and his pickaxe and everyone laughed, then the men fell to making plans for their trip on the following day until Jason said: 'I'll carry Letitia indoors, I think, she doesn't want to get chilled.' He got up in leisurely fashion. 'Where is she to go?'

'The sitting-room—we'll have drinks, shall we? No, better still, take her straight up to her room, will you, so she can pretty herself up, then you can bring her down again.' Georgina looked at Letitia. 'You're not tired, Tishy?'

'Not a bit—how could I be? I've been here all day doing absolutely nothing. It's been heavenly, but I feel an absolute fraud.'

'Until you try to stand on that foot,' remarked Jason, and picked her up. 'Back in ten minutes,' he told her as he lowered her into the chair before the dressing table in her room and went away at once. She barely had the time to pick up her hairbrush before Georgina came in. 'Don't try and dress,' she advised, 'or do anything to your hair,' and when Letitia eyed her doubtfully: 'You look quite all right as you are.'

She went away too, so Letitia brushed her hair and creamed her freckles and sat quietly, not thinking of anything very much until Jason came to carry her downstairs again.

The evening was one of the best she could remember, for she felt quite at ease with Georgina and Julius, and as for Jason, his easy friendliness made her oblivious of her appearance and she even forgot her freckles. She reminded herself that two months ago, out with Mike, she would have been fussing about her hair and wondering if her nose were shining and whether she had on the right dress. With Jason it didn't seem to matter; he hardly looked at her, and when he did it was in a detached way which didn't once remind her that her hair was loose and a little untidy, and her gown, though charming, was hardly suitable for a dinner party. He carried her up to bed presently and before he left her took a good look at her ankle.

'Quite OK,' he pronounced, and wished her goodbye, because he and Julius would be leaving very early the next morning.

The house, after they had gone, seemed large and empty, a fact to which Georgina agreed, giving it her opinion that it was because they were two such large men; all the same, the two girls contrived to spend a pleasant day together, with Stephens and the gardener to carry Letitia down to the garden and the two babies to play with. Julius telephoned twice, the first time shortly after they had arrived, and the second time a few hours later, just as the girls were going to bed. Letitia wondered what Jason was doing, but she didn't like to ask Georgina, who, for some reason, didn't mention him at all, but when Julius telephoned the next morning, she couldn't refrain from asking at what time the men might be expected back.

'Well, there's no telling,' explained Georgina. 'They both drive fast and awfully well and I daresay they'll take it in turns, which means that they'll do it in about six hours. They can do seventy on the motorway, you see, and that's almost all the way. They'll be here for tea.'

And she was right. Letitia was entertaining Polly with a demonstration of 'Here's the church, here's the steeple' when she heard men's voices and looked up to see them strolling towards them. Neither looked in the least tired, although they ate an enormous tea.

'No lunch?' asked Georgina.

'Well, my love, I had promised myself that we would be home for tea,' Julius smiled at his wife, 'and Jason liked the idea too.'

Letitia watching them, thought how wonderful it would be to be loved as much as that. She sighed, and Jason asked at once: 'Are you tired? Do you want to go indoors and rest?'

She shook her head. 'No, oh, no, thank you.'

His voice was kind. 'One more day and then I should think you might try some gentle exercise. How does the ankle feel?'

She hardly noticed when the others went indoors and Jason started to tell her about Edinburgh and their meeting. She was surprised when Julius came out to ask them if they wanted to go in for drinks before dinner. The day, though pleasant, had been long, now the evening was going far too quickly.

The next few days went quickly too, each one speedier than its predecessor, or so it seemed because she was enjoying herself so much. It was a week after her accident, when she had been hobbling very creditably for a couple of days, that Julius gave her his verdict that she was to all intents and purposes, cured. Jason wasn't back from hospital, she was sitting with Georgina and him, lingering over tea, watching Polly tumbling around on her short fat legs, and thinking how content she was. But it couldn't last, of course; she said at once: 'Oh, that's good. Do you think that I should go straight back to St Athel's?'

'Lord, no, Tishy. A week's leave—you can stay here if you care to—we love having you.'

She smiled at them both because they were so kind and they must have wished her out of the way on occasion. 'You're awfully kind,' she told them, 'but I'd love to go home. If I could have a lift up to town I could catch a train. Would you think me very ungrateful if I went tomorrow?'

'Yes, very,' said Julius promptly. 'Make it the day after.' He smiled as he spoke. 'Do you want to collect more clothes before you go?'

'No, thanks, I've some things at home—they're a

bit old, but I shan't be going anywhere, so it won't matter.'

So it was settled, and when Jason came home nobody thought of mentioning it to him and she didn't like to say anything herself, although presumably, as Julius was still on holiday, it would be Jason who would have to give her a lift. It wasn't until the next morning, after he had left the house, that Georgina remarked: 'Oh, by the way, Jason says he'll take you all the way, Tishy, if you don't mind leaving quite early in the morning.'

Letitia buttered a piece of toast and sat looking at it. 'I couldn't let him do that,' she said at length. 'I mean, it's miles away, even in that car of his.'

It was Julius who answered her. 'Well, he'll be home after tea, why don't you talk to him about it then? And if you'd really rather go by train, he can still give you a lift up to town.'

So she was forced to contain herself until the early evening, for Jason was late home. By the time he strolled in they were all in the drawing room with the children in bed and dinner but half an hour away. Julius got up to get him a drink. 'A bit of a rush?' he wanted to know.

'The Commando went wrong—he picked up eventually, but it lost us a couple of hours, we didn't finish until six o'clock.'

Georgina glanced at the carriage clock on its bracket. 'You made good time.'

He had taken a seat at the other end of the sofa where Letitia was sitting. 'The car went well.' He looked at Letitia. 'How far to Chagford, dear girl?'

She jumped because she hadn't expected his question. 'Well…yes, the thing is Georgina told me…it's very kind of you to offer me a lift, but I really can't…if you wouldn't mind dropping me off at Paddington…' She stopped, aware that she wasn't making much of a success of it.

'I think you've got it wrong,' explained Jason, at his most placid. 'I'm going down to Plymouth tomorrow—I have to. I might just as well take you as not—the car's empty and I'm not going more than a few miles out of my way. It's no sacrifice on my part, Letitia.'

She told herself that she was relieved to hear that even while a faint prick of annoyance shot through her; would it have been such a sacrifice if he had been asked to drive her down to Chagford? Probably; he had called her touchy, hadn't he? And damned sensitive, too—and he had wanted to go to sleep instead of talking to her. That still rankled a little. He must find her incredibly dull after the glamorous young ladies he was doubtless in the habit of escorting. She said in a wooden voice:

'Well, thank you, I'll be glad of a lift. When do you want to start tomorrow?'

'That brings us back to my question. How far to Chagford?'

'A hundred and eighty-seven miles from London.'

'A good road?'

She frowned in thought. 'Well, I don't know it very well. It's the M3 and then the A30 for the rest of the way, more or less.'

'Good enough. We'll go round the ring road and pick up the motorway on the other side of London. Leave at nine sharp? You'll be home for tea.'

'It's quite a few miles to Plymouth from my home,' she reminded him.

'That's all right, Letitia,' he told her pleasantly. 'I enjoy driving, it makes a nice change from theatre, you know.'

'That's settled, then,' said Georgina comfortably. 'Let's have dinner, Mrs Stephens has made a special effort by way of a farewell gesture to you, Tishy, so we mustn't spoil it.' She turned to Jason. 'You'll be back in a day or two, won't you? Spend a day or two here on your way home.'

'Thanks, George, but only an hour or so—I can't expect Bas to do my work and his for ever.'

'You do his when he goes on holiday, but I know what you mean. Still, we'll see you when we come over on holiday.'

'Of course. Julius and I might even get in some sailing.' A remark which triggered off a conversation about boats which lasted through dinner, and although the talk became general afterwards, Letitia, on her way up to bed an hour or so later, discovered that beyond casual remarks which she could count on the fingers of one hand, Jason hadn't talked to her at all. She went to bed a little worried, for it augured ill for their journey the next day. Would they travel in silence, she wondered, or should she attempt to entertain him with lighthearted remarks about this and that? It was a great pity that she knew nothing about sailing and not much about fast cars. And it would bore him to talk about his work. She was still worrying away at her problem like a dog at a bone when she at last fell asleep.

CHAPTER THREE

IT WAS A glorious morning and bade fair to be a hot day; the tan jersey suit was going to be far too warm before very long. Letitia wished she had something thinner to wear, until she saw that Jason intended travelling with the BMW's hood down. She prudently tied a scarf over her hair, assured him that she liked fresh air, bade her friends good-bye and got into the seat beside him, eyeing the restrained elegance of his cotton sweater and slacks; he was a man who looked elegant in anything he wore, she considered, blissfully unaware of the price he paid for such elegance.

'Warm enough?' he wanted to know, and when she said yes, nodded carelessly and with a last wave took the car down the drive, past the little lodge and into the lane. 'Nice day for a run,' he observed, then lapsed into silence. Now would be the time, thought Letitia, when she should embark on a sparkling conversation which would hold him enthralled, but there wasn't an idea in her head, and the harder she thought, the emptier it became.

'Ankle all right?' asked her companion, and she embarked with relief on its recovery, her gratitude to Julius and Georgina and himself, and how much she had enjoyed her stay at Dalmers Place. But even repeating herself once or twice couldn't spin her colloquy out for ever; she lapsed into silence once more, looking at the scenery with almost feverish interest in case Jason should imagine that he might be forced to entertain her.

They were slowing down to go through Epping when he said blandly: 'This erstwhile young man of yours—did he train you to speak only when spoken to?'

She was instantly affronted. 'What a perfectly beastly thing to say! Of course not. I—I can't think of anything to talk about, if you must know.'

'Dear girl, I'm in the mood to be entertained by the lightest of chat, and surely you're used to me by now—Big Brother Jason, and all that.'

She laughed then and he said at once: 'That's better. I thought we might stop for coffee before we get on to the motorway—Windsor, perhaps, with luck we should be able to lunch in Ilminster, unless there is anywhere else you would prefer?'

She shook her head. She didn't know of any restaurants as far-flung as that; when she had gone out with Mike he had taken her to unpretentious places where he always made a point of assuring her that the food was good however humble the establishment appeared to be. She suspected that his ideas of good food weren't quite in the same category as Jason's; certainly the hotel where he chose to stop for coffee was a four-star establishment, the kind of place Mike would have considered a great waste of money. She savoured the luxury of their pleasant surroundings and began to enjoy herself. Jason was a charming companion and amusing and not in the least anxious to impress her. They went on their way presently, nicely embarked on the kind of casual talk which demanded very little effort and allowed for the maximum of laughter. Letitia hardly noticed the miles as they slipped by under the BMW's wheels, and when they stopped in Ilminster, she said regretfully: 'How quickly the time has gone!'

The doctor smiled gently, remarking merely that he was hungry and hoped that she was too as he ushered her into the George Hotel. 'See you in five minutes in the bar,' he suggested, and left her to tidy her wildly untidy hair and re-do her face. The freckles were worse than ever, she noted with disquiet, and then decided to ignore them; Jason had said he liked them.

The hotel was a pleasant place. They had their drinks and then ate their lunch with healthy appetites; cold roast beef, cut paper-thin, with a salad so fresh that it looked as though it had just been picked from the garden, and a rhubarb pie which melted in the mouth to follow, accompanied by enough clotted cream to feed a family of six. They washed down this splendid meal with a red Bordeaux and rounded everything off with coffee before taking to the road once more, making short work of the miles to Exeter, and once through that city and out on to the Moretonhampstead road, with the hills of Dartmoor ahead of them, they slowed down so that they might miss nothing of the scenery around them.

Somehow it didn't surprise her to learn that the doctor had been that way before, she suspected that he was a man who got around quite a bit without boasting about it—all the same, she was able to point out some of the local sights as they went along, and when they had gone through Moreton-hampstead and slowed down still more to go through Chagford, she told him about the Grey Wethers stone circle close by before directing him to turn off the road and take a winding lane leading off towards the heart of the moor.

'It's such a small village that it isn't on all the maps,' she explained, 'and the road isn't very good, although a few people use it when they want to see Yes Tor, but most of them go from the Okehampton road, it's easier.'

Her companion grunted and dropped to a crawl; the lane had become narrow and winding, sometimes passing through open wild country with enormous views, and then dipping into small, densely wooded valleys which defied anyone passing through them to see anything at all.

'We're almost there,' offered Letitia placatingly as Jason swung the car round a right-angled bend, 'and you won't need to come out this way; there's a good road over the moor that will get you on to the Tavistock road.' She pointed down into the valley running away to their left. 'There's the church.'

The lane became the village street with a scattering of cottages on either side before it widened into a circle with an old-fashioned drinking trough for horses in its centre. The church lay ahead with the rectory alongside, a wicket gate separating its garden from the churchyard, past which the road wandered off again, up the hill on the other side. Jason, still crawling, afforded Mrs Lovelace, who ran the village shop and post office, and was the natural fount of all local gossip, an excellent opportunity of taking a good look at both him and his beautiful motor-car as he turned into the rectory gateway, slid up its short drive and stopped soundlessly before its porch.

The garden had appeared to be empty, but all at once it was full of people; her father coming round the side of the house to meet them—a middle-aged, rather portly man, of medium height and with a cheerful face, and her mother, who rose, trowel in hand, from the middle of a clump of lupins ornamenting the herbaceous border, and four girls, all pretty, who came tearing out of the door to cluster round the car.

Letitia cast a lightning glance at her companion and found him to be as placid as usual, only his brows were raised a little and a smile tugged at the corner of his mouth.

The introductions took quite a few minutes and the doctor bore up under them with equanimity. They were out of the car by now and Letitia, having made Jason known to her parents, started on her sisters.

'Margo,' she began, 'back from Scotland, I daresay you've seen her at St Athel's, and Hester, she's married to a doctor in Chagford, and Miriam who's married to a vet in Moretonhampstead, and this is Paula, who's still at school.'

He shook their proffered hands and submitted to a battery of eyes without appearing to mind.

'A little overpowering,' murmured the Rector as Letitia was drawn, with a lot of talking and laughter, into the family circle. 'So many women—of course, I'm used to them, bless their hearts, but they might possibly strike terror into a stranger's heart.'

The doctor laughed: 'Hardly that.' He turned round to look at them, gathered in a charming bunch round Letitia. 'You must be delighted to have them all home together,' he observed to Mrs Marsden.

She smiled at him, a small, still pretty woman.

'Yes, it's wonderful, and it happens so seldom. How kind of you to bring Letitia home—such an unfortunate accident...'

'I was the cause of it, Mrs Marsden.'

She shook her head. 'But not to blame; Letitia wrote and told me exactly how it happened; it was hardly your fault that she was pushed into the road.' She looked with interest at the BMW. 'It's a beautiful car, Doctor...' she wrinkled her nose, 'I'm so sorry, I've forgotten your name.'

'Jason.'

She smiled at him. 'Such a nice name. You'll stay to tea?'

'I'd like to very much.'

'That will be delightful,' observed the Rector, who had joined them silently. 'You and I will be able to hold a rational conversation and let these featherheads gossip themselves to a standstill.' He beamed at his visitor. 'Do come inside—are you by any chance interested in porcelain? I have one or two pieces of which I'm very fond, they are in my study...'

'Tea first,' decreed his wife firmly. 'Perhaps afterwards, if Jason has time.' She turned to look at the doctor. 'You're more than welcome to stay the night, we have any number of empty rooms.'

'I should have liked that, but I have to be in Plymouth this evening, but perhaps I might call on my way back and be shown the porcelain?'

'Splendid—I shall look forward to it,' his host agreed. 'And now—tea.'

They had the meal round the large rectangular table in the dining room, because, as Mrs Marsden explained, they had never quite got used to the idea of just a cup of tea and a biscuit. 'When they were younger, the girls had long cycle rides to and from school and always came home famished, and the Rector usually finished his visits about half past four or five, and somehow, even though all the girls are away from home, excepting Paula, we keep to the old habit.'

If the doctor found a table spread with a starched white cloth, plates of bread and butter, scones, little dishes of jam and cream, a variety of small cakes and a large fruit cake only waiting to be cut, a little different from his own idea of tea, he said nothing— indeed, he made a hearty meal, equally happy discussing eighteenth-century soft paste figurines with the Rector and the pleasures of living in rural surroundings with his hostess, while goodnaturedly answering the questions the girls put to him—all but Letitia, who was a little silent; it had just struck her that she was unlikely to see him any more. He had only taken over Julius's work at St Athel's to oblige him, and Julius was due back—he would go back to his own country and become, in time, a vague someone she half remembered. Even while the thought crossed her mind, she knew that wasn't true; Jason wasn't someone easily forgotten. She longed to ask him what he was going to do in Plymouth, and when Paula, who had no inhibitions about asking personal questions when she wanted to know the answers, asked just that, Letitia listened with both ears, while at the same time gazing attentively at her mother, deep in a tale about repairs to the organ.

'What are you going to do in Plymouth?' Paul asked with shattering directness.

'I have to meet someone.' The doctor's voice was mild.

'I bet it's a date—or are you married?'

He laughed at her, not in the least put out. 'You might call it that, and no, I'm not yet married.'

The word yet worried Letitia. Did that mean that he was about to get married? It seemed likely, and she was a little surprised to find that the idea didn't please her at all, which, for a girl who had recently broken her heart over another man, seemed strange, especially as she neither liked nor trusted men— young men—any more, although he had assured her in the most avuncular fashion that he had no interest in her, hadn't he? which meant that she could like him without changing her ideas... She frowned and then smiled when he spoke to her. 'I'm coming back this way in a couple of days, Letitia—just for an hour or so. Will you be here.'

'Oh, yes—I'm not going anywhere.'

He nodded. 'Good. If your ankle is up to it, you shall show me some of your beloved tors.'

'You could see them just as easily from Plymouth,' pronounced Paula. 'With that car of yours, it would only take you…' she paused, 'though perhaps it would be wasting your time—I mean, you can see a for any time you're this way, but if you've got a date…'

She was frowned and shushed into silence. 'Oh, all right, I won't ask any more questions and I'm sorry if I was rude—I was only trying to save your time; Tishy knows the country round here awfully well. She goes about looking in hedges and badgers' setts and birds' nests and things—she'll be better as a guide for you than anyone else I know, and if you're not stuck on her, you'll pay more attention to the tors, won't you?'

This outrageous speech brought a choked back laugh from the doctor, a surge of colour to her knowledgeable sister's cheeks and a chorus of protest from everyone else. When it had died down Mrs Marsden said apologetically: 'I'm sorry that Paula has been so rude. I don't think she meant to be impertinent; the trouble is that in these days the young are encouraged to speak their minds.'

Jason's face was calm and placid once more. 'Don't apologize, Mrs Marsden. I have a young sister myself and I'm quite accustomed to her expressing herself in much the same way.' He smiled at Paula, who grinned back, quite unrepentant. 'Have you any more brothers or sisters?' she wanted to know.

'Four other sisters,' he told her with a twinkle, and the rest of the girls, but not Letitia, chorused: 'Five of them—just like us.'

Letitia found four pairs of eyes turned on her 'Tishy, you didn't tell us.'

'I didn't know.'

'Oh, Tishy darling—' it was Paula again, 'why didn't you ask? I know you don't like men any more, but Jason's used to girls—I mean sisters, if you see what I mean.' She smiled in a kindly way at Letitia, who was fuming silently. 'I expect he thinks of you as a kind of sister—and sisters ask questions,' she shot a look at Jason. 'Don't they?'

She looked round the table triumphantly and her father remarked dryly: 'I think it must be very nice for Jason to have five sisters, but I wonder if they annoy him sometimes?'

'Oh, frequently. Luckily the four eldest are married so their husbands get the lion's share of them, and I don't see a great deal of Katrina, the youngest.'

The talk became general after that and not long after Jason declared that he would have to go. Everyone went outside to see him off with a great deal of waving and a host of instructions as to the best way to go, and a reminder that he was to call in on his way back. Letitia watched him drive away, her temper still doubtful, for he had said almost nothing to her other than the briefest of good-byes; she went back indoors with her sisters, feeling peevish.

But it was impossible to feel put out for long; she hadn't seen any of them, save Margo, for some time, and there was a great deal to talk about. The evening flew by, and when she went to bed she was so tired that she went to sleep as soon as her head touched the pillow. And in the morning she had no chance to be by herself, even if she had wanted it. Margo was going back to St Athel's after lunch, and before she went she wanted to hear all the latest news of Georgina and the hospital too, and now that Paula had gone off to school and Miriam and Hester had gone to their own homes, they had the time for a talk while they did the household chores together.

The house seemed very quiet after Margo had gone, Letitia left her father to work in his study and joined her mother in the garden. It was a gloriously hot day, and Letitia lay back on the grass, aware that the sun was playing havoc with the freckles again, while her mother's gentle flow of conversation eddied and flowed round her head; it was the kind of conversation which needed almost no answering, and Jason wasn't mentioned once.

She borrowed her father's car the following day and drove her mother into Chagford to have coffee with Hester, and then on to Moretonhampstead to have lunch with Miriam and admire the baby. It was almost tea time when they left, and that evening her mother had to attend the Women's Institute, which meant that Letitia got the supper ready while she was away, played a rather one-sided game of chess with her father, and took Shep, the old retriever, for his short evening amble. She thought she wasn't in the least tired when she went to bed, but she slept at once, to wake to yet another lovely morning. Her ankle felt fine again and there was nothing for her to do at home; a walk would be splendid and perhaps resolve the puzzling restlessness she seemed unable to shake off, so that when her mother suggested that she might like to go for a ramble up towards Yes Tor, she was more than ready to agree.

Half an hour or so later, the washing up done and the beds made, she set off, wearing old slacks because of the brambles, and a cotton shirt which had seen better days, and because there was no one to see, she had simply tied her hair in a ponytail.

Her path led her away from the road which ran

through the village, and presently it wasn't a path at all, but a well-worn track running over grass and heather. It plunged presently into a charming little wood which filled the whole of the valley between her and the tor. She would sit there, she promised herself, before climbing the hill on the other side. She meandered along, looking where she was going because of the ankle, and wondering at the back of her mind why Jason hadn't telephoned to say when he would be coming; perhaps he had thought better of it—perhaps the date Paula had asked about really was a date, after all. Had he imagined that she would stay at home every day in the hope that he would come, or didn't he mind if he never saw her again, despite his friendly suggestion about the tors? She was uncertain—that was Mike's doing; he had said one thing and meant another, and for all she knew Jason was like that, too.

She was half-way through the wood, looking for somewhere to sit, when she saw the boy. He was lying a few yards from the path, on his stomach, his head turned sideways away from her, resting on his arms. A gipsy, she guessed; they often spent a few days tucked cosily in the valley and nobody minded, for they were only a small party of two or three caravans and bothered no one. She said hullo as she passed him, slowing her steps in case he woke up and wanted to talk, but he didn't answer. She walked on and then stopped. Supposing he wasn't asleep? He could be ill—dead even. She went quietly through the bracken and bent over him. He wasn't asleep, but neither did he see her properly. His face was white and his eyes, half open, were clouded. She knelt down beside him and took a closer look. Here was a very sick boy, and in a high fever; she wondered how long he had been there and why no one had come to look for him, and when she took his pulse it was far too rapid and when she felt his skin it was hot and dry. She would have to get help; it would mean leaving him lying there, but there was little chance of anyone coming along the track—she might wait all day.

The gipsies usually camped down by the little stream which ran through the wood at the bottom of the valley, where it branched away towards the open country again; Letitia had passed the rough grass track between the trees only minutes before. If he had come from there, the chances were that they hadn't missed him yet. She took a last worried look at the boy and ran back along the path and down the track. It led steeply downhill, winding and uneven between the trees, until it resolved itself into a delightful small clearing, with the stream skipping and rushing over the grey stones of its bed, and the trees encircling it, so that everything was shaded and cool, and but for the birds, very quiet.

She had been right; the caravans were there—two of them, with a little tent pitched between them, the horses hobbled close by and a lurcher dog tied to a caravan wheel. It barked when it saw her, but the bark sounded appealing more than menacing, and when she called 'Hullo there!' no one answered at all. She stood still for a moment, wondering what to do, when she caught a faint sound from the caravan furthest from her. A little nervously she crossed the grass and knocked on the open door, and when she heard the sound again, went in. It was dark inside and very hot and smelly too, and amidst the furniture crowding its interior, an old man lay on a bunk bed against one wall. He was ill too; even in the half-dark she could see that. She said at once in her practical way: 'Hullo—you're not well, are you? What can I do to help?'

He muttered and mumbled at her and finally waved a feeble arm towards the door. 'The other caravan?' she asked, and he nodded.

It was as crowded as the first one, more so, because here were two people, a youngish man and a woman. The man appeared to be unconscious, but the woman, Letitia was relieved to see, looked as though she might be strong enough to talk.

'How long have you been like this?' Letitia asked her gently.

The woman stared at her, blinking uncertainly. 'A day—two, I don't know.'

'The boy—I found a boy. Is he yours?'

The dark eyes came alive for a moment. 'Yes—he's ill too? He went to find someone.'

'Listen,' said Letitia, 'I'm going for help—I shan't be long, can you hang on for a little longer? My father will get a doctor to come...'

'The parson?'

'That's right. I'll see to your son too. Don't worry.' She looked around her and found what she was searching for; water, cooled in the kettle—a great black kettle dumped on the floor under a table. She filled a mug and gave some to the woman, then wetted the man's lips before she crossed to the other caravan and gave the old man a drink too. Then she fetched a pan and filled it with water for the dog—the beast would be starved as well as thirsty, tied up like that. Her eyes lighted upon a hunk of cheese on the table; she snatched it up and offered it to the poor creature, who demolished it in a couple of gulps. The horses would need attention too, but they would have to wait a little longer. She started back up the track, going as fast as she could.

Where it joined the main path she paused. Perhaps she should get the boy to the caravans first and make him as comfortable as possible before she went for help, but with all the will in the world, she knew she couldn't do it; he was far too big for her to carry, and to drag him over the rough ground would be madness—besides, her ankle, though mended, might not stand up to such treatment. She turned to the right, in the direction of the village, barely a mile away.

The sight of Jason, coming along between the trees at a steady, unhurried pace, would have filled her with surprise, but all she was conscious of was relief. She said desperately: 'Oh, there you are—what a mercy!' She gulped deeply, being still short of breath from her haste. 'They're all ill—the gipsies—and there's a boy.' She waved an arm behind her. 'The dog's starving too, and there are two horses…'

She felt his hands, firm and reassuring, on her shoulders. He didn't waste time repeating her not very clear remarks, nor did he ask what she meant by them. He asked in a calming voice: 'Where are they? Take your time—it will be quicker in the long run.'

He was right; Letitia took several long, steadying breaths. 'Down that track—there's a small clearing at the bottom, there are two caravans there. The boy's along this path—I think he's unconscious.'

'Lying on the path?'

'No—to the left, a few yards from it, you can see him…'

She felt herself pressed gently down on to a fallen tree. 'Sit there. I'll get him first, then you can show me where the others are.'

Letitia sat, suddenly tired, wondering if she had dreamed it all. But not the boy, at any rate; within a very few minutes she saw Jason coming back, the boy in his arms. As he reached her, he said in an easy voice: 'Now, dear girl, lead the way,' and she started off down the track once more, but more slowly this time because though Jason was a giant of a man, the boy he was carrying must have been quite heavy.

They reached the clearing without mishap, and the dog, hopeful of more food, strained at its chain and barked its head off. The old man opened his eyes as Letitia went into the caravan and mumbled something as the doctor laid his burden down on the second bunk.

'The boy first,' said Jason, and took off his jacket and cast it through the door on to the grass outside. 'The others are in the caravan over there, I suppose?'

'Yes—do you want me here?'

'Not for the moment—see if you can get a kettle of water going, they need cleaning up, and perhaps you can cool some it for them to drink—boiled water can't do them any harm, whatever it is.'

She nodded wordlessly and crossed over to the

larger caravan, found another kettle, already half filled with water, and set it on a Primus stove. There were a great many dirty cups and plates about too; she collected them up and piled them into a tin bowl and carried them outside; presently she would wash them up. She found a bucket too and fetched water from the stream, then gave it rather awkwardly to the horses before beginning a hunt for something to give the dog. The cupboards were well enough stocked with food; she selected a packet of Rich Tea biscuits and a tin of corned beef, mixed them together on a plate and laid it before the dog, who polished it off with delight, washed it down with more water, and then allowed her to take him off his chain, tie a length of rope to his collar, and fasten him to a nearby tree, where he lay down at once and fell asleep.

The kettle was on the boil when she returned and as the woman was dozing still, she went to see what the doctor was about, for it seemed to her that he was being a very long time.

The caravan seemed hotter and gloomier than ever as she went in, and smaller too by reason of his size, but he had got both of his patients out of their outer garments. They lay in a smelly heap in one corner and he was bending over the boy.

'There you are!' he exclaimed, his tone implying that she had been somewhere or other enjoying herself. 'I wish I had my bag with me. We'll have to get help as quickly as possible, I fancy. Can I leave you to get these two reasonably clean and give them a drink? And throw out as many clothes as you can, will you? I'm going to have a look at the others.'

She did as he had bidden her, although to get the occupants of the caravan really clean was beyond her, but at least she bathed their faces and hands and unearthed fresh blankets before she tossed their discarded clothing out on to the grass. She was barely finished when Jason joined her. 'The woman's not too bad,' he told her. 'The man needs attention as soon as possible; he and the boy and the old man must have been ill for several days. The woman told me that there's another caravan expected this evening. I think the best thing we can do is to get this lot to hospital, get the place cleansed and wait for the arrivals. They might be able to take over the animals—they're friends of these people, I presume.'

It was a relief to have someone there, making decisions in a calm way. Letitia nodded. 'I'll go and wash the other two,' she told him. 'The old man has a rash on his chest, but you'll have seen that.'

She went to pass him, but he caught her by the arm and swung her round to face him. 'Yes, dear girl. Typhoid.'

'Ty...oh! Are they bad?'

'If you mean are they going to die, no, I don't think so—not if we can get them to hospital within a reasonable time.' His hand was still on her arm. 'Have you by any lucky chance had a TAB injection lately?'

'Yes, a month ago—we had a carrier on the surgical wards.'

'Splendid, so you're safe.' He took his hand away and gave her a little push. 'Off you go to your tasks. I'm going back to your home to ask your father to telephone the local doctor and arrange for someone to stop the other caravan when it comes. You'll be all right here?'

'Yes. Jason, no one's had typhoid...' Her eyes were a little worried, though her voice was as matter-of-fact as his.

He smiled reassuringly. 'I shall stand by the gate and bellow,' he told her, 'then I shall come straight back.' He turned away. '*Tot ziens.*'

She had no idea what that might mean, but it sounded cheerful. She called ''Bye,' and made her way over to the second caravan, and presently, armed with more warm water and soap, began her work. The woman, when her face had been bathed and her hair tidied and she had been got into a clean garment, looked hearteningly better, but the man hardly stirred. Letitia gave them both a drink and went to see how her other patients were faring. The old man was still muttering, but the boy looked a little better. She went outside again and added the clothes from the other two to the pile on the grass and went to put on another kettle, giggling a little as she did so; it reminded her of an old film, where invariably in an emergency hot water was called for, whether it was needed or not. Now there was no emergency any more, only a need for her to wash her hands. A cup of tea would have been welcome, but there was nothing safe to drink from. She was drying her hands on the seat of her slacks when Jason came back, and it wasn't until she saw him coming towards her that she realized just how glad she was to see him again.

CHAPTER FOUR

HE WAS CARRYING his bag under one arm and she recognized the family picnic basket in his hand. In the other he held a small suitcase. He put it and the picnic basket down under the trees and came towards her, moving with a calm air of purpose which she found reassuring. 'Hullo,' he greeted her. 'What pillars of strength your parents are. Your mother had the basket packed within five minutes—you've had no lunch, have you? Sit down now and eat something and drink the tea.'

'I'm quite all right,' she began.

'I know that, but do as I say, or you won't be of much use later on when there'll be work to do. Your father telephoned the local doctor; he's on his way. Once he's seen these poor souls, we can get them away.' He started towards the caravans. 'I'm going to take another look—go and eat your sandwiches, and save a cup of tea for me.'

She was glad of the food and still more of the tea, but she wasted no time on her scratch meal. Five minutes later she was beside Jason as he examined the boy once more. He looked round as she sidled past the table and chairs and cupboards. 'Your Doctor Robinson has asked for a couple of ambulances; it's going to be quite an exercise getting the four of them down to the road, but once they're away the third caravan can come in and take over the animals while the Health people get these places fumigated.' He nodded towards the pile of clothing outside. 'I'm afraid that lot will have to be destroyed.'

Letitia was giving the old man a drink. 'Father has a stock of clothes he keeps, he'll fit them out again. The jumble sales, you know.'

The doctor looked a little at sea, but it was hardly the time to go into the manifold blessings of the village jumble sale—besides, she could hear footsteps. They belonged to Doctor Robinson, who greeted her with the freedom of an old friend and edged past her to join Jason. Presently the two men went over to the second caravan, to join her after a few minutes.

'No doubt of it,' pronounced Doctor Robinson, 'it's typhoid all right. Luckily you happened to come this way, Tishy, and luckier still that you have had your TAB so recently. I've just been suggesting to our good friend here that you should both go to the Isolation Hospital and get cleaned up.' He eyed Letitia's person. 'Nothing smart you mind parting with, I daresay? All old stuff?'

She was on the point of replying when Jason said: 'I asked your mother to put a few things in a case

for you—you can change in the hospital, and leave
that stuff to be burnt.' His tone implied that it should
have been burnt months ago, so that when she
asked: 'And what about you?' her voice was tart.
How dared he criticize her clothes; that her slacks
were a bit shabby she was bound to admit and the
cotton shirt had seen better days, and neither had
been improved during the last few hours, but what
could it matter to him anyway?

'Oh, I've a change of clothes,' he told her carelessly. 'Perhaps you would make sure that they're
more or less ready to go?'

His voice was that of a consultant asking a nurse
on his ward to carry out his instructions; kindly, distant and polite. Letitia found herself obeying. She
was rather despairingly searching for some sort of
nightwear for the boy when she heard voices and
the tramp of purposeful feet, and peered round the
door to see the clearing suddenly full of men—am-
bulance men, clad in protective clothing, bearing
stretchers. They started about their business with
cheerful competence, and one by one the patients
were strapped to their stretchers and borne away,
leaving the two doctors, the horses, the dog and herself.

'They'll be along to get this lot cleaned very
shortly,' observed Doctor Robinson. 'They'll take

you along in one of their cars, I daresay—can't offer you a lift myself, I'm afraid.'

'The animals,' said Letitia, not caring a great deal as to the arrangements suggested. 'I won't go until there's someone to look after them—I'll wait until there's someone…I daresay they'll be here before the caravans are sealed.'

To her surprise Jason agreed with her. 'That dog looks as though it could do with some exercise and I need to stretch my legs. I'll free the horses too and then get them tied where they can get at the grass.'

'The dog won't understand,' persisted Letitia, aware that she was being childish about the animal.

'Probably not, but I'll talk to these gipsies when they get here—and his boss won't be away all that time, you know. Typhoid isn't the long-drawn-out business it used to be now that we have Chloramphenicol.'

'Yes…I was just wondering if I could have him at home with me—I know I have to go back in a day or two, but Paula will look after him and Shep and Bossy won't mind. Do you suppose he would stay?'

'Probably. There's no harm in trying—the boy could collect him when he's better.'

Doctor Robinson closed his bag. 'Well, I'll be on my way—you two will be all right?' He shook hands with Jason, pinched Letitia's cheek and started off along the track. Before he disappeared from view he turned to call: 'I'll tell those men to hurry themselves if I should meet them.'

He was barely out of sight when Jason declared that he would see to the horses at once and then attend to the dog. 'Well, I'll start getting the caravans ready for the men,' declared Letitia, ever practical. 'Empty cupboards and drawers and get the canned stuff out of the way—the rest of the stuff will have to be dealt with, I suppose?'

'I should imagine so. Do you want any help?' He had picked up a bucket and was already walking away from her. She said 'No,' because in the circumstances it would have been silly to have said 'Yes,' the question having been rhetorical. She plunged into the nearest caravan and worked with such a will that by the time the men arrived she had almost cleared the second one as well. Of the doctor there was no sign; presumably he had gone with the dog. She went forward to meet the Health team, uncertain as to what she should do next; when he appeared silently from the thickly growing trees at the side of the clearing, the dog at his heel. From then on she had no need to do anything; he seemed to know exactly what was needed, what had to be done, and who was to do it, and while he made no attempt to interfere in any way Letitia could see that he was regarded as being in charge of the business.

It was late afternoon by now and she was hungry again as well as longing for a cup of tea. The men worked fast, though; presently they declared themselves satisfied with their work and prepared to go.

'And you go with them, dear girl,' Jason advised her. 'Take your case with you—I'll wait until these other folk arrive, arrange about the horses and see about the dog.'

There was something in his voice which made her say 'Yes, Jason,' in a meek voice of her own, pick up the case and join the Health team. One of the men took the case from her with a cheerful: 'Come along, miss,' and she found herself walking away beside him, the other men trailing behind her, while their leader stopped to speak to Jason. She wondered, as she went, when she would see him again—perhaps she wasn't going to. The thought stopped her in her tracks; she wanted to see him again. Just once more, she pleaded silently, even if he calls me dear girl in that offhand voice and doesn't really look at me—if only I were pretty, he might...

She followed the men up the track, feeling lightheaded—probably, her common sense told her, because she was so empty inside, but her heart gave her another reason: she had fallen in love with Jason Mourik van Nie, and although common sense pointed out that she couldn't have done anything sillier or more unsuitable, her heart would have none of it. Common sense at times could be a dead bore, said her heart, and love was often silly and unsuitable and sometimes hopeless. As long as she remembered that and started, without waste of time, to forget him, not much harm would have been done. The thing was to be practical about it and use her good sense. Her father had always said that she was the only one in the family blessed with that commodity; now was the time to prove it. She plodded on, not feeling in the least sensible, longing to relieve her pent-up feelings with a good cry.

She saw him two hours later; he was waiting for her outside the hospital, leaning up against the BMW's sleek bonnet and talking to one of the doctors, but he saw her as she walked through the door and as the other man walked away called: 'Over here, dear girl—what an age you've been, though I must say the result seems worth it.'

She had wondered how she would feel if and when she saw him again, but she had imagined nothing like the wild rush of feeling which caught at her breath, but she snatched at the remnants of it and said sedately: 'I'm sorry if you've been waiting, I didn't know...'

He looked surprised. 'You didn't imagine that I should leave you stranded here, did you? I did what was necessary and managed a lift back to your home to fetch the car.' He smiled at her, his eyes crinkling

into little wrinkles at their corners. 'I like the out-
fit—and the hair's very smart, even though it does
turn you into a young lady.'

What had he considered her to be before, for
heaven's sake? she wondered crossly; she had only
washed it and coiled it in its usual knot on top of
her head, and as for the dress, there was no knowing
why her mother had chosen to pack the flowered
cotton shirtwaister which she had been keeping to
go to church in—it was the only decent thing in her
wardrobe at the rectory, except for the jacket and
dress she had travelled in, but at least she felt clean
once more.

Jason opened the door. 'Jump in,' he invited, and
she jumped.

The BMW made short work of the journey to the
rectory, and beyond a number of observations con-
cerning the gipsies, and his assurance, in reply to
her question, that the third caravan had arrived, had
parked on the edge of the wood, had taken the
horses into its owner's care, and had handed over
the dog without demur for the time being, the doctor
had little to say. And nor had Letitia; she had too
much to think about.

They were accorded a welcome fit for heroes and
led indoors into the dining room, where the lurcher,
a little bewildered, sat in an old box, being sized up
by Shep and Bossy the cat. 'I've a meal ready,' ex-

claimed Mrs Marsden. 'You must be famished, the pair of you. Sit down, do, and when you've finished you can tell us all about it—what excitement—those poor souls...' She departed kitchenwards, her voice becoming fainter and taking on strength as she returned with a tureen of stew, its fragrance filling the pleasant old-fashioned room. She bade her husband fetch the vegetables and began to ladle their supper into plates, an act which the lurcher found sufficiently encouraging for him to sidle forward, eyeing Shep and Bossy warily. 'Presently, my dear,' Mrs Marsden admonished him. She sounded absent-minded; she had just noticed the expression on Letitia's face and wondered what had happened to put it there.

'You'll stay the night, of course,' she bade the doctor in a motherly voice. 'Such a pity Paula is at Miriam's she would have loved to have seen you.'

'May I? I had intended to cross on the midnight ferry. I could drive through the night, of course...'

'Out of the question, Jason—you know you're tired, you need a good night's sleep. Leave as early as you like in the morning. We're early risers and in the summer it's no hardship to get up with the sun.'

'How kind you are.' Letitia, her eyes on her plate, was aware that he was looking at her. 'If I could leave before seven o'clock? I could go through Dover; it's a good deal nearer.'

'Which way do you usually go?' asked the Rector.

'Harwich, it's convenient for Dalmers Place.'

Letitia looked up. 'Are they expecting you? Shouldn't you telephone?'

He was making great inroads into his supper. 'I would be grateful if I might do so.'

'And arrangements about your crossing tomorrow?' the Rector wanted to know. 'I'll take my chance.' Jason smiled at his host. 'I shall have time to look at your porcelain after all, sir.' Which meant that after supper he disappeared into the Rector's study, the dogs in attendance, and Letitia saw nothing of him until bedtime, and that for a brief moment only, when he wished her good night and good-bye at the same time, with the observation that he would be gone before she was up in the morning, and that in a cheerfully casual tone which precluded her from saying more than that she hoped that he would have a good journey. She even smiled at him with false brightness and thanked him once more for doing so much to help her, but all the answer he gave was: 'Ah, but I didn't see the tors after all, did I?'

Letitia wakened very early and lay listening to the familiar little sounds the old house made in the quiet-hours; creaks and sighs and the occasional tip-tap of small mouse feet behind the wainscoting. Neither she nor Bossy, who had chosen to sleep on the end of her bed, took any notice of these faint noises; they were too used to them, but they both sat up at the sound of almost silent footsteps crossing the landing and going downstairs. Jason, already up.

Presently Letitia heard his voice, very quiet, in the garden, and when she peeped from her window it was to see him going down the drive, the lurcher on a makeshift lead, Shep trotting with them. She could dress quickly, go downstairs and get his breakfast—she was on the point of doing just that when she remembered that he had evinced no strong desire to see her again; indeed, he had taken it for granted that she wouldn't be up so early and had made no effort to persuade her to do otherwise; she remembered, too vividly, his careless good-bye. It would serve him right she decided pettishly, if her mother overslept and he got no breakfast at all, but this uncharitable wish was stymied; she heard her mother go downstairs and soon after, the sound of Jason's return. There was nothing for it but to go back to bed.

Letitia sat up against the pillows, listening to their distant voices, and sniffing at the delicious smell of bacon coming from the kitchen. In a little while she heard Jason in the garden again and then the click of the BMW's door. He was going—she scrambled

from her bed and ran to the window, just in time to
see the car's stylish back disappear through the rectory gate. The wish to throw wide the window and
yell at him to come back was very great; there was
so much she wanted to tell him—that he had helped
her to recover from Mike, that she liked him, that
she would miss him. She would be able to say none
of these things now; that she wouldn't have said
them in any case was a small point she chose to
ignore. All that mattered was that he had gone.

'Don't be silly,' she told herself sharply, and because bed was impossible now, wandered downstairs in her nightie and barefooted, to perch on the
kitchen table and drink tea with her mother. She
wanted to talk about Jason, but didn't; instead she
plunged into plans for going back to St Athel's with
a fervour which deceived neither her mother nor herself. Though both ladies were well aware that that
wasn't what she wanted to talk about, Jason wasn't
mentioned once.

The day went slowly by, following the exact pat-
tern of all the Sundays Letitia could remember at
home. Church, breakfast, church, lunch, then help
with Sunday School and Evensong to finish the day.
Not that her father expected her to attend all the
services; all he asked was that one member of the
family should be there. She shared the day with her
mother, because Paula wouldn't be home until after

tea, and sat quietly through Matins, listening to her father's voice and the enthusiastic singing of the surprisingly large congregation, and admiring, as she always did, the carving on the rood screen, and all the while her thoughts were miles away, with Jason Mourik van Nie, driving his BMW back to his own country. And Holland to Letitia, who had never travelled outside the land of her birth, might just as well have been darkest Africa or Cape Horn, all equally unreachable.

She spent her last day at home picking raspberries, helping Paula to cut out a dress when she got back from school, and cleaning, with great care, her father's small collection of figurines. Jason had liked them, her parents told her happily; what was more, he had known what he was talking about. 'A knowledgeable young man,' went on the Rector as he watched his daughter at work. 'I should like to know him better—he's quite an expert on Coalport, you know.' He added wistfully: 'It's a pity he lives so far away.'

Indeed it was a pity, agreed Letitia silently, and said aloud: 'Yes, Father.'

'You won't be seeing him again?' he inquired of her.

'No, dear—he only came to St Athel's to take over from Julius while he took a holiday.' She made her voice light and disinterested, and beyond declaring that it was a great pity that such a promising acquaintance should come to an end, her father said no more. She applied herself to the cleaning of a much prized Shepherd Boy with Dog and allowed her thoughts without any effort at all, to return to Jason.

Back in hospital, she found the next few days difficult; for one thing the recovery room without the possibility of seeing Jason from time to time had become, for the moment at any rate, positively dull. She did her work with the high standard of efficiency demanded of her; she saw the patients safely into theatre and then, after the surgeons had dealt with them, received them back again and encouraged them to regain consciousness once more, aided by all the latest gadgets science could devise, and once they had opened their eyes she gave them something to ease their pain, waited for their blood pressure to become normal once more and then saw them safely back to their wards. It was a busy way to spend a day, and never two days alike. Each patient was different and needed different things done for them; she was kind and gentle and absolutely reliable, but behind her calm she felt terrible; it was as though part of herself had gone with Jason—the important part, leaving only the outside of her, the part that showed, to go on working and eating and talking and trying to sleep at night. It began to show

in her face and her friends were forced to admit
amongst themselves that Tishy had become decidedly plain just lately, and some of them thought she
might still be pining for the Medical Registrar.

She was aware that her modest looks were suf-
fering. She spent more time than she had ever done
before on her make-up, but that didn't help much.
It was Margo, meeting her on her way to dinner,
who expressed sisterly concern for her appearance.

'You look as though you need a good holiday,'
she remarked, 'even though you've been home. As
it happens George wrote today asking me down for
my days off and wondering if you could come with
me. You always have Saturdays and Sundays, don't
you? OK, I'll give myself a week-end and we'll go
down to Dalmers Place next week-end. How's the
ankle?'

'Fine,' said Letitia, trying to make up her mind if
she wanted to go, and added, unable to prevent herself. 'Will there be anyone there?'

'Lord, yes. It's George's birthday—we'll have to
get a present.' She frowned in thought, then went
on: 'Cor and Beatrix and Franz and the older one,
Karel, will be there too, but I don't think Dimphena
can get over until next week, but that Jason Mourik
van Nie is bringing his youngest sister over—it
should be fun. Have you got anything to wear,
Tishy?'

'No,' said Letitia instantly, seeing this as a sign from heaven that she wasn't to go and not sure if she were glad about that or not. Seeing Jason again would be wonderful, but it would be awful too. She wouldn't go. This worthy determination was knocked for six by her sister's next remark, though. 'Not to worry, I've some money tucked away and you can pay me back later. What do you need?'

'Nothing—that is, I don't think I'll go, Margo.'

Her sister gave her a considered look. 'George will be very hurt if you don't, and she'll be bound to find out, because Julius would tell her.'

'Well,' said Letitia reluctantly, 'in that case... I've got that tan thing and the blouse, I could go in that, couldn't I? I left that pretty shirtwaister at home—a pity. I haven't anything to wear in the evening, though there's that blue crêpe that Miriam couldn't get into because of the baby...'

'That thing?' Margo sounded scornful. 'We'll do better than that, love. Are you off at four?' and when Letitia nodded: 'Good, meet me in my room as soon after that as you can manage, we'll go shopping.'

They found what they wanted; a plainly cut silk voile with an elegant line to it, in a pretty pale green, and because it was a little more than Margo had intended to pay, they pooled what money they had and found a coffee and white striped cotton dress, a straight sheath into which Letitia's nice little figure fitted very well. 'No one needs to know where it comes from,' Margo pointed out as they hurried back to the hospital. 'It looks marvellous on you and they'll never guess that we got it at the British Home Stores, and you've got that lovely suede belt that will go with it exactly.' She gave a satisfied little nod. 'You'll look lovely, Tishy.'

Letitia thanked her eldest sister and said she hoped so, all the while knowing that her hope that Jason might find her lovely was just too silly for words. But the green dress was very pretty—he might at least look at her. She remembered the casual glances he had cast in her direction; perhaps this time he might look, really look at her.

They met the next morning and he hardly glanced at her on his way into theatre, striding through the recovery room with a casual 'Hullo, dear girl,' and not waiting a second for her to reply. Not that she had anything ready to say; she had been taken completely by surprise; she had had no idea that he was in England, let alone anaesthetizing that morning. She stood holding a recovery tray in much the same manner as a Grecian girl holding an urn, her mouth slightly open. Then she snapped it shut and almost dropped the tray as Julius strolled through in his turn. He stopped, however, wished her good morning as though he really meant it, and expressed pleasure at her impending visit. 'Nice to have a few friends from time to time,' he remarked. 'How's the ankle?'

She told him that it was fine, remembering that Jason hadn't bothered to ask, then flushed under his kindly eye. 'You look as though a couple of days off would do you good,' he commented as he went on his way.

It was to be a busy morning with a long list, being added to every now and again as emergencies came in, and Letitia was kept busy, but not so busy that she didn't see Jason each time he came into the recovery room, and each time she couldn't help but notice and he was going out of his way to be friendly, so that by the end of the morning she was on top of her small world again. To come plummeting down again at the end of a long, hot afternoon.

She had gone into the little cubbyhole where they washed the instruments and replenished the trays and trolleys. Mrs Mead had already gone, the room was quiet after the day's ordered bustle, she stood leaning against the sink, still filled with odds and ends which needed to be washed and dried and thought about Jason being so nice—he had been like that at Dalmers Place when he had told her he was like an uncle…she wished, upon reflection, that he hadn't said that, perhaps when he saw the new green dress…her thoughts were disturbed by the swing of the theatre door and the deliberate tread of feet.

She had thought that the men had all gone, but it was Julius's voice:

'Coming back for dinner, Jason?'

'Good of you, old man, but I've a date.'

'With Tishy?'

Jason's careless: 'Lord, no,' seared her like a hot iron. 'Wibecke van Kamp is over here, you know—we're dining together.'

'Good-looking girl—knows how to wear her clothes too.'

'Handsome, I should have said.' Jason's voice was dry, and in the little pause which followed Letitia summoned up the courage to walk out and let them know that she was there; eavesdropping was a rotten, low-down trick and none knew it better than she, being a parson's daughter, but she was halted by his voice. 'How's Tishy? She looked a bit down in the mouth when I got here this morning.'

'Well enough, I should imagine—she and Margo are coming down for the week-end. She'll be glad to find you'll be with us as well, I think.'

'What makes you say that?'

'You've been kind to her, and she needed kindness after that young fool cut her up—for a little while she's been hating all of us; he said some pretty cruel things to her, so Georgina told me. It can't be

much fun to have your dreams torn up so ruthlessly—and it must have been worse for a girl like
her.'

'No looks, you mean?' It was Jason's voice, and
Letitia closed her eyes. 'But she's not as plain as all
that, you know, and she's a nice girl.'

'That's just what I mean,' observed Julius. 'There
aren't many around like her any more.' They were
strolling to the door now. 'Where are you dining?'

Letitia didn't hear Jason's reply because the door
had swung to behind the men, but it would have
made no difference. She had become deaf and blind
and dumb for a while while her head buzzed with a
variety of painful thoughts, which changed, within
seconds, to sudden rage; he was as bad as Mike had
been—worse, because he hadn't seemed like that at
all. True, he had never been in the least interested
in her, but why had he pretended to be friendly when
all the while he hadn't meant it?

She began on the sink's contents, making such a
clatter that the theatre staff nurse came out to see
what was the matter, and when she got off duty at
last, her cross face kept even the closest of her
friends at bay, so she was left to brood over a book
and peck silently at her supper, a circumstance so
unusual that the young ladies around her looked at
her with something like dismay; little Tishy was
known for her sunny disposition and no one had

ever seen her quite like this not even when Mike had thrown her over.

And the efforts she made to get out of going with Margo were useless; she didn't choose to tell her sister her real reason for not wishing to go to Dalmers Place, and the excuses she thought of wouldn't hold water with Margo. She got through Friday somehow, wishing Jason a good morning cold enough to freeze his bones when he arrived for the first case, and carrying out his instructions and giving him her reports of the patients' conditions in an austere manner which caused the faithful Mrs Mead to look at her as though she were out of her mind. It was at the end of the list, after everyone had gone and Letitia was setting the recovery room to rights in case an emergency should come in during the week-end, that Jason came back again. And this time she was in the middle of the room, rotating slowly, making sure that everything was just so before she left.

'Ready in half an hour, Letitia?' he asked her cheerfully. Obviously, she thought pettishly, her coolness of manner had escaped him, and what business was it of his when she left? Margo had told her that they were going down by train and would be met at the station.

'No. There's plenty of time before Margo and I leave, doctor.'

He raised faintly amused brows. 'I'm not sure what I've done, but it can't be so awful that you need to call me doctor. What's up, dear girl?'

She said levelly, her eyes on his face: 'Nothing—nothing at all. It was quite a list, wasn't it?'

Either he had never heard of red herrings or he wasn't easily led away from the matter in hand. 'Well, whatever the nothing is, you'd better get over it; it's George's birthday tomorrow.'

Letitia went a slow pink, a pale indication of the indignation burning inside her. 'I hadn't forgotten.'

'Good.' He glanced at the clock. 'Twenty minutes, then, at the front entrance—Margo already knows we're going down together.' He smiled quite kindly and went away, leaving her to rush round to the Home. Margo could have let her know; she would have something to say to her when they met. Letitia changed in an increasingly bad frame of mind and got to the entrance with one minute to spare, to find Jason and Margo, on the best of terms, already there, so that, naturally enough, she was ushered into the back of the car where she sat with her thoughts, answering politely when spoken to and trying not to look at the back of Jason's head, which, while not as interesting as his handsome face, had its own endearing qualities. The gay talk and laughter of the two in front of her did nothing to make the journey pleasanter, either.

And when they arrived the house seemed full of people. Georgina, of course, looking so glowingly happy that she was beautiful, and Julius, looking as he always did, completely content, and with them his cousins, Cor and Beatrix and Franz with an ecstatic Polly weaving amongst them on her short legs, and there were two people Letitia had never meet before too—Julius's eldest cousin Karel and a pretty girl of fifteen or sixteen, Katrina, Jason's youngest sister. They were swept indoors with everyone talking at once, and presently Letitia and Margo were taken up to their rooms, warned that dinner would be in half an hour or so and left to unpack while they talked to each other across the communicating bathroom.

'Don't change,' Georgina had told them, as she went. 'No one will tonight—we're going to dress up tomorrow evening, though.'

A remark which filled Letitia with disquiet because she wasn't sure if the green dress was grand enough after all.

She went downstairs with Margo in a little while and joined everyone in the drawing-room, and because she wanted to avoid Jason, she went to sit by Franz, and presently Karel joined them. He was a dear, she discovered, gay and amusing and with the happy knack of making her feel that she was the prettiest woman in the room, a feeling which she recognized as entirely false though it helped enormously, so that when Jason did come over with his sister she was able to laugh and talk in a perfectly natural manner—so much so, indeed that when they went in to dinner, he bent his head to whisper: 'So the nothing's gone, has it?'

Which brought it all back again even though she pushed it to the back of her mind and prepared to enjoy herself. It would have been difficult to have done otherwise; she had Cor, bubbling over with schoolboy high spirits, on one side of her, and on the other Karel; between them they kept her entertained throughout dinner, and afterwards, in the drawing room, she found herself with Katrina, who was so very like Paula in her ways that she felt they had known each other for a long time and readily agreed to go for an early morning walk with her before they parted, on excellent terms, to go to bed.

It was going to be a blazing hot day, Letitia could see that the moment she wakened the next morning, and a good thing too—now she could wear the British Home Stores dress. It really wasn't bad at all; the good suede belt lent it an air and her sandals, on bare feet, matched quite well. She tied her hair back and without bothering overmuch about her face, went silently through the rambling old house and down the stairs.

Katrina was already there in the hall, they found

their way to a side door and let themselves out into the garden, and although it was barely seven o'clock, it was already warm. They wandered along out of the garden presently and into the lane with Katrina, talking all the time, leading the way. They had gone perhaps half a mile when she stopped and exclaimed in a pleased voice: 'There is Jason!' and there indeed he was, sitting in the hedge ahead of them, chewing grass and contemplating the view. He threw the grass away and got to his feet and came to meet them. His good morning was bland. 'Now this is a surprise,' he assured them, only he didn't look surprised at all.

CHAPTER FIVE

JASON TOOK IT for granted that they would enjoy his company, and as a matter of fact, it would have been difficult to do otherwise; he could be very amusing when he wished and he and Katrina were on excellent terms with each other despite the difference in their ages. They strolled back to the house across the fields, and when Jason said: 'Run on ahead and tell Georgina we're on our way,' Katrina obeyed at once, flying away from them over the grass, turning to wave as she disappeared through the gates leading to Dalmers Place. Which left Letitia making uneasy conversation with Jason, something she found difficult enough to do, partly because she couldn't forget his cool voice in the recovery room, and when he said in his kind way: 'I like that dress, Letitia,' she felt sure that he was mocking her; it was a dress, that was all. To her mind it had bargain written all over it, she couldn't believe that her companion wasn't able to recognize a cheap garment when he saw one.

'It's from British Home Stores,' she snapped, and realized that he had no idea at all of such a place. Well, she thought fiercely, it was time he learnt. 'It's

97

a chain store, like Woolworth's,' she informed him crossly, 'they have rows and rows of dresses, all exactly alike and all very cheap.'

Jason had stopped to look at her and twisted her round to face him. He said in a measured voice. 'It doesn't really matter if it's sack or something dreamed up by Christian Dior—the point is, it's pretty. In fact it has the edge on some of the ultra-fashionable clothes I'm expected to admire.'

'Whose?' she asked before she could stop herself.

He grinned down at her. 'Well, well—I was beginning to think you had no interest in my—er—leisure hours. I take girls out sometimes, you know—men do.' He put a finger under her chin so that she couldn't turn away from his blue gaze. 'And we aren't all men like Mike, my dear.'

He bent to kiss her cheek gently, tucked an arm under hers and went on walking towards the house, talking about a variety of small matters, for all the world as though they had never stopped. She mumbled answers and said yes and no and was glad when they went indoors and she could escape to her room and tidy herself for breakfast. She stared at her face in the charming winged mirror; his kindness had hurt. Which was perhaps why she devoted so much of her attention to Karel at breakfast and played tennis with him for the greater part of the morning. And after lunch on the terrace, when Georgina had received her presents, she had spent the afternoon with Katrina and Karel with occasional games of tennis with Beatrix and Cor. It was evening when the celebrations really got under way; Letitia dressed in the green silk, nervous that it wasn't quite up to the occasion, and though when she got downstairs she saw that it wasn't, it didn't matter overmuch, because its very simplicity made it look better than it actually was and she was wearing the gold chain and locket her parents had given her when she was twenty-one—it was a large Victorian oval, heavy and rather ornate, and showed up nicely against the plainness of the dress and gave it an air of distinction.

Georgina, in guipure lace and the emerald earrings Julius had given her, was holding court in the drawing-room, and as she and Margo went in there was a burst of laughter which carried her well through drinks and into dinner. She had Karel next to her again and he stayed with her when they all went back to the drawing-room, introducing her to the guests who were beginning to arrive for the evening, and when someone put on the music, he whisked her on to the floor before she had had a chance to wonder if anyone would dance with her. She didn't lack for partners after that, for she danced well. Only when she found herself with Jason did her feet become clumsy, but presently, charmed by the music and the pleasure of dancing with him, she forgot her awkwardness and enjoyed herself.

'That was nice,' she told him as the music stopped last, and smiled up at him, almost pretty in the dim light of the wall sconces, but before he could answer her she had been danced away by Karel, to circle and sway and twirl in a very modern fashion which seemed a little surprising in the strictly brought up daughter of a country parson. But it didn't prevent her watching Jason revolving round the room in a rather more civilized way with a pretty girl whose hair was golden and whose dress must have cost the earth. They disappeared into the garden very soon, and Letitia dipped and swayed and smiled her way through the endless dance, longing to run after them and see what they were doing. There was a moon and the evening was warm—the garden was lovely; sweet-smelling and romantic, and the girl was the kind of girl men would kiss in the moonlight. She ground her nice white teeth at the very idea; if he asked her to dance again, she would refuse. Only he didn't ask her, and when the evening was over and they were all going to bed, his good night was so casual it sounded like an afterthought; rather as though he had forgotten to say good night to the dog, she decided bitterly.

Everyone went to church in the morning; a convoy of cars, headed by Julius's Rolls, followed by the BMW, the Mini driven by the just seventeen-year-old Franz and last, the rakish Porsche belonging to Karel, in which Letitia had contrived to get herself as passenger. They filled two pews in the little church, and Letitia, squashed between Beatrix and Karel, was very aware that Jason was sitting beside her, so that instead of attending to the service she was worrying about her hair being untidy at the back and whether the collar of her jacket was just so. Being in love, she mused silently while they sang the last hymn, was an uncomfortable business.

They had a noisy lunch and then, because it was such a glorious day, decided on a picnic tea. Letitia, changing into the British Home Stores dress, meditated on the advantages of being rich; no need to worry about cutting sandwiches or hunting for paper bags and rugs; Stephens, summoned by Georgina, had listened attentively and with his usual fatherly air, and had disappeared with his habitual quiet, and when they gathered in the hall later, there, just as she had guessed, were the two picnic baskets and two rugs, folded neatly. The men shared them out amongst themselves and the girls started off ahead of them, Polly between Cor and Beatrix, Georgina and Margo behind them and Letitia and Katrina bringing up the rear. They were making for the meadows, a quarter of a mile away, where they sloped down to a small stream, a copse guarding the hill behind them. It was pleasant there and cool, and the ladies of the party spread the picnic, while the men got the spirit kettle going and the children wandered off to look for fish in the stream. It was all very peaceful and Letitia, arranging slices of cake on a plate, wished it could go on for ever.

The picnic was a tremendous success, largely because it owed nothing to the modern aids of thermos flasks, cellophane-wrapped sandwiches and potato crisps. Georgina made the tea in a large brown teapot and Margo cut bread and butter with a bread knife on a bread board, just as though she was in a kitchen and not kneeling on the grass. And Letitia, having seen to the cake, unwrapped a jam sponge for the children and a pot of Gentlemen's Relish for the men, then started to dole out the strawberries into little glass dishes. The cloth, spread on the grass, looked very inviting, they clustered round it in great good spirits and ate everything there was before packing up in a leisurely fashion with a great deal of laughing and talking.

'I shall have a nap,' declared Julius, and stretched himself out and closed his eyes, while Georgina wandered off with Polly. Letitia, getting to her feet after strapping the picnic baskets, caught Jason's eye on her and spoke hastily. 'I thought I'd...' she began.

'Go for a walk?' he interrupted her. 'I'll come

with you.' He had her hand in his and was marching
her away before she could think of anything to say.
She was still cudgelling her brains for a safe topic—
something impersonal—the weather, perhaps?—as
he led her up the field towards the copse which
crowned it. Unlike her, he showed no signs of un-
ease at their lack of conversation; he said nothing at
all, only wandered along, with her in tow, whistling
under his breath. A rough track led left and right
away from them when they gained the copse, cir-
cling the field on its outside, and facing them was a
gate; still silent, Jason fetched up against it, and Letitia perforce stopped too.

From where they stood the view was charming;
all the soft sweep of the country beyond. The gate
gave access to a large, irregular field with a hump
down its middle, so anyone walking along either of
its edges would fail to see anyone or anything on
their opposite side until they were almost at the top
where the ground levelled out once more. They
stood side by side, silently contemplating the scene
until presently they saw Georgina and Polly climb
the narrow little gate halfway down the field, and
start rambling towards them, keeping close to the
hedge.

They saw the bull seconds later, his great head
raised, standing on the other side of the hump, sniffing the air. He began to move towards the centre of

the field, unhurriedly but with purpose, aware that
there were strangers in his field, although he wasn't
able to see them because of the hump. As he began
to amble up his side of the hump, Jason said quietly:
'George won't hear us if we shout, we're too far
away. Go and fetch Julius, dear girl, tell him to run
down the hedge on that side and get George and
Polly through the gate. I'll stroll down the middle
and hold the beast's attention.' He turned to grin at
her. 'Possibly he's quite harmless, but we can't take
risks, can we?'

Even at that distance, Letitia considered this de-
scription of the noble animal's disposition to be
quite inaccurate; he was plodding slowly up his side
of the hump still, looking anything but harmless, but
she wasted no time in saying so, only turned and
ran as Jason vaulted over the gate.

She ran well, and being country bred, found the
stones and tree roots and unexpected bumps in her
path no obstacle—besides, it was downhill. All the
same, she was breathless when she reached the picnic party, rather scattered by now, but Julius was
still there. He looked up in astonishment at her head-
long flight and was on his feet before she got to
him, tugging his arm with an urgent hand.

'Jason says come at once,' she said breathlessly.
'There's a bull—George and Polly...'

'Show the way,' Julius urged her, not stopping to

ask questions, but Letitia, needing no urging, was already starting back the way she had come. At the gate once more she paused. 'Jason said would you go down on that side—' she waved an arm, 'and get them through that little gate half-way down while he heads the bull off.'

Julius nodded, vaulted the gate in his turn and began to run towards his wife and little daughter, still pottering slowly along the hedge. Letitia could hear their laughter now, faint still, mixed in with the birds and the other summer sounds.

Jason was well down the other side of the hump now and the bull had stopped to look at him, and George and Polly had paused because they had seen Julius. Letitia, from her vantage point at the gate, thought Jason was getting dangerously close to the bull now and he had quite a long way to run back too, and it was uphill; he would never do it. She went cold inside as she turned to see how Julius was getting on. He had snatched up Polly and had Georgina by the hand and was racing back to the little gate; everything was going to be right after all, just so long as the bull stayed where he was.

But he didn't—he tossed his great head, then lowered it and advanced at a sharp trot; he didn't think much of Jason, who moved back up the hump to make sure that the others were safe, and they were; it remained only for him to get himself away. Letitia knew then that he would never do it; the bull, with nothing else to occupy his mind, was bent on reaching him as quickly as possible. She climbed the gate neatly and began to run down the hump so that the beast would see her too. He was still some distance away, but she didn't like the way he stopped in his tracks when he caught sight of her and changed course in her direction. But the small distraction had given Jason the chance he needed, he had gained the crown of the hump and was racing towards her. She turned and ran too, breathless with fright, quite sure that she would be able to get over the gate before the bull reached her. But she need not have worried; Jason caught up with her within yards of it, picked her up and tossed her over it as though she had been thistledown instead of a healthy girl, and leapt after her.

She had fallen softly enough into grass and rather mushy weeds; he plucked her to her feet and brushed her down, but the front of her dress was stained and ruined; Letitia thanked heaven that it had been so cheap and when he asked her if she was all right, nodded, staring at him because, incredibly, he was laughing. And he was only a little out of breath too, whereas she had almost none at all, and what she had she lost in a gasp of fright as the bull fetched up within feet of them, only on the other side of the gate. He glared at them for a moment, then tossed his head and strolled away, and Letitia's gasp turned to a weak giggle.

Jason laughed again, a great shout of laughter, and turned her round to face him. 'Dear girl,' he said, 'dear brave girl,' and bent to kiss her.

Sudden tears filled her eyes. 'Oh, Jason,' she wailed, 'I thought...'

She managed to stop herself just in time as he put an avuncular arm round her shoulders and gave her a gentle hug, and presently, when she gave a resolute sniff, took out his handkerchief and mopped her face for her. And only just in time, for Julius came round the bend in the path to halt and say:

'You're all right, both of you? I can never thank you enough.' He smiled at them both, his face white and strained. 'Polly found it all quite fun.' His eyes slid over Letitia's blotchy face. 'Though I can't say I did. I left Georgina sitting in the hedge having a little weep, but I had to make sure you two were all right—we saw you running like hares.'

'A nasty moment,' agreed Jason, 'and if it hadn't been for our Tishy here I don't think I should have made it.' He took his handkerchief from her hand and gave her a little push. 'Run down the path to George,' he suggested, 'we'll follow,' and when she hesitated: 'Go along, Letitia, we'll explain to the others.'

She went then, grateful to him for realizing that

she wasn't in a fit state to answer a barrage of questions for the moment. The rest of the party had been on the other side of the stream when she had fetched Julius; she could hear them now, pounding up the path, eager to help. She heard Karel's: 'I say, what's up?' as she rounded the bend in the path and saw George with Polly on her lap. Polly was singing to herself and her mother had finished her little weep. 'And if only,' said Letitia to herself, 'I could look like that when I cry, instead of puffy and red.' She went and sat down in the hedge too, saying brightly: 'My goodness, what a scare! I'm still shaking—and I howled all over Jason, too.' She added: 'He was laughing!'

Georgina smiled a little. 'Men do the strangest things sometimes. You were so quick and brave, Tishy. Thank you, both of you,' she kissed Letitia's cheek. 'Weren't you afraid?'

'Terrified, and I should never have known what to do—it was Jason. I didn't know Julius could run like that.'

'Julius can do anything,' stated his wife simply. 'But you and Jason—I can never thank you enough…' She broke off at the precipitate arrival of Cor and Beatrix who flung themselves upon her with cries of: 'George, darling George, are you all right? Julius sent us to look after Polly so's you can rest a bit.'

The two girls watched the children go, this time with a delighted Polly between them. 'Dear Julius,' said Georgina, 'I expect he thinks I'm still crying.' They smiled at each other and Letitia said: 'You don't look a bit as though you had. I expect I'm still blotchy.'

'Only a little, and I don't think anyone will notice—sometimes men don't see things which we think matter frightfully.'

They got to their feet presently and followed the children, to join the group standing by the gate, and after the episode of the bull had been well and truly discussed they all wandered down to where they had had the picnic, and everyone sat down again and talked about it still more. Karel had attached himself to Letitia and his light, cheerful chatter made her laugh a good deal as well as serving to soothe her jumpy nerves, but even while she smiled at his jokes she was wondering why it was that Jason had wandered off with Cor and Franz, with no more than a smile for her.

Presently they began to wander back to the house in twos and threes, to change for the evening before meeting in the drawing room for drinks. Letitia and Margo were to be driven back to St Athel's later that evening, and although no one had actually said so, she had taken it for granted that it was to be Jason who would drive them, but when they came down to the hall, it was Karel who was waiting for them, and going the rounds, shaking hands and murmuring nothings. Letitia, offering a hand to Jason, could see no sign of disappointment on his face. Indeed, he wished her a good journey, assuring her that Karel was just the companion to make the drive a pleasant one. He made no mention of seeing her again either, so that she said hesitantly: 'Well, I hope you have a good journey too, you and Katrina—it was nice meeting her, I shall tell Paula all about it when I go home.'

Letitia stared into his impassive face, longing to say a great many things she knew she would never utter. 'Good-bye,' she said at last, and when he replied: '*Tot ziens*', she turned away with a puzzled face and promptly embarked on a gushing conversation with Franz, who looked taken aback but was too polite to show it.

She sat in front with Karel this time and he kept the conversation going at a rate which rivalled his speed, and made her laugh a good deal as well. And when they arrived at the hospital and he suggested that she might like to spend an evening with him, Letitia agreed, mainly, as she admitted to herself later, because there was a chance that he might talk about Jason. They parted on the friendliest of terms, and as she went with Margo to the Nurses' Home, her sister remarked: 'What a nice boy he is,' and added innocently, 'You get on very well together, Tishy.'

Letitia pushed the door of the home open and they went in together. She said 'Yes,' suddenly beset with the appalling thought that perhaps Julius, or worse, Jason, had told him to be nice to her. They climbed the stairs to the first landing, where Margo had her room in the Sisters' wing, whereas Letitia was two floors higher. 'Tishy,' began her sister, 'Jason and I were talking—he has a plan; did he tell you about it?'

Letitia mumbled a no and managed a yawn. She didn't want to talk about him. She was still sore from his casual good-bye; she didn't like him at all even while she loved him so fiercely. 'I'm tired,' she declared, 'and I'm on early in the morning— won't another time do to tell me? I don't suppose it's important.'

'Not really,' Margo gave her a thoughtful look. 'Tishy, I was beginning to think you'd got over Mike; that you'd discovered that he was the bad apple in the barrel, but I'm not so sure.' She kissed her lightly. 'Poor little Tishy!'

'I'm perfectly all right and I've quite got over Mike,' declared Letitia peevishly, and at the same time wondered what Jason and Margo had been planning together. She wished Margo good night and went to bed, telling herself that the quicker she got him out of her system the better.

Impossible, because he was there the next morning, going unhurriedly across the recovery room to theatre, bidding her a cheerful good morning as he went. She gaped, muttered incoherently at him and then busied herself laying a tray which was already laid: she simply had to do something to cover the wave of delight which had engulfed her; not that it would have mattered if she had allowed her feelings to show, for he didn't pause for one second, but disappeared through the doors without a second glance. Letitia didn't see him again until he came out to inspect the first case an hour or more later; a gastrectomy that wasn't looking too good. They worked on the man together, silent save for Jason's brief directions, and when the patient was fit enough to go back to the ward, he went back into theatre with the smallest of nods.

And so the day wore on, with their dinner cut short because an emergency Caesarean was rushed in as the last case went down. The theatre filled rapidly; students, another doctor to see to the baby and a nurse to see to the doctor, the surgeon and his assistant. Sister and a handful of nurses—and Letitia, waiting quietly by the door, ready to take over the patient, her eyes on Jason, giving the anaesthetic. She had been with him when he had given the pre-

liminary injection and started the anaesthetic, placidly reassuring towards his patient, talking in a quiet
voice as he popped the needle in so that the anxious
young woman smiled as she closed her eyes. Letitia
remembered that now as she studied his bent head—
but only for a moment, for the baby was there and
everyone was smiling broadly, as they always did
when there was a Caesar in theatre. When the small
creature gave a peevish whimper, she sighed with
relief in unison with everyone else there. There was
something dramatic about a Caesar and satisfying as
well.

Letitia took charge of her patient again, and when
she had come round, stood back so that Mr Toms,
the surgeon, could announce the news that she had
a son before Letitia saw her back to the ward. After
that there was the tidying up to do before she could
rush down for some sort of a meal. She gobbled it
as fast as she could and raced back; the afternoon
list was due to start in five minutes and Staff Nurse
Wills, who usually relieved her, had an afternoon
off, leaving Mrs Mead and her to cope. The list
wasn't a long one, thank heaven, so she got back,
still chewing, with seconds to spare.

They were finished by half past four, and the last
case had been obligingly quick in regaining consciousness once more, so that soon after five o'clock
Mrs Mead was on the point of leaving, and Letitia,

slapping instruments into their proper places with brisk efficiency, was trying to decide what she would do with her evening. Not much, she decided; she had very little money in the first place and what she had she must save so that she could go home on her next days off—she liked to go once a month, even though it meant going without puddings at dinner and the cinema. She would wash her hair, she decided, do her smalls, make a pot of tea and eat the rest of the biscuits she had, then have a leisurely bath before the others came off duty, and get into bed early with a book. She placed the last airway into its correct position and skipped along to the changing room. Jason was leaning against its door, looking like a man who had never done a day's work in his life. He picked a thread off the sleeve of his elegant suit and said: 'Hullo, I've been waiting for you, Letitia.'

'Me?' It sounded stupid, but she couldn't think of anything else to say.

'You.' He smiled and her heart turned over. 'Will you have dinner with me, dear girl?'

'No,' said Letitia.

He sighed. 'I'm not supposed to be here, you know,' he pointed out with patience, 'but something went wrong yesterday, didn't it?—before then, perhaps. You closed up like a clam—I was rather looking forward to the week-end at George's, but you had iced over…only when you came charging to my rescue at the picnic did you forget whatever it was. What was it, Letitia?'

He put out a hand and plucked her theatre cap from her head, so that her hair stood out in untidy wisps around her face. 'Remember I'm only an uncle type—you can tell me.'

'No,' repeated Letitia, fighting a desire to fling herself at him just as though he were an uncle—that was the last thing he was.

'Something someone said,' persisted Jason, just as though she hadn't spoken. He watched her face. 'Something I said—ah, now we have it! Tell me, dear girl. It will be quicker, you know, for I intend to stay here until you do.'

She took a quick look; he meant what he said. She took a deep breath and keeping her eyes on his face, began: 'I was here—last week, when you and Julius came through after the list. You were going out to dinner with someone called Wibecke. I was at the sink,' she jerked her head backwards, 'behind that door, and I was going to come out so that you would know that I was there, only before I could, you said…' She paused, not because she had forgotten a single word of it, but so that she might steady her voice.

'I remember exactly what we—what I said; that

you were a nice girl and not as plain as all that.' He spoke gently, his eyes very intent.

She looked away at last. 'That wasn't as bad as the bit before. You said "With Tishy?" as though the very idea appalled you, and now you've got the cheek to ask me out to dinner with you.' Her voice was bitter and regrettably wobbly. 'Are you doing penance or something?' She choked on her rage and when he put out a hand and turned her face to his, she tried to pull away.

'No, don't do that, Letitia,' he spoke firmly. 'I'm sorry you overheard what I said, but get this into your head—I wasn't appalled, only very surprised. You see, I had been warned that you were off men for the time being; it never occurred to me that you would agree to come out with me even if I had asked you, and I didn't know you very well then, did I? and I've known Wibecke for years. And as for the rest: you are a nice girl, and you aren't all that plain—you grow on one, you know, and one day you will grow on some man so much that he'll discover that you're the prettiest girl in the world for him.' He smiled down at her. 'You're a little goose, and I've been clumsy and I'm more sorry than I can say. I should like to take you out very much. The offer,' he added gravely, 'is being made entirely without pressure or suggestion from any one else.'

It was weak of her to give in—she knew that. He

thought of her as a nice, plain girl, he had just said so, quite safe to take out and unlikely to raise his pulse by a single beat. But she knew that he was a friend, when he added: 'Wear that pretty green dress, dear girl,' she said quite meekly: 'Very well, Jason.'

CHAPTER SIX

BECAUSE IT WAS still early in the evening, he took her to a restaurant which catered for theatregoers, Le Gaulois in Chancery Lane. She had read of it in the glossy magazines but she had never expected to see it from the inside. Jason ushered her in, explaining: 'We're not going to a theatre, but we can talk here in peace and eat early.'

It was a small place and very French, already more than half full as they were shown to their table. When they were seated, Letitia asked in a small voice: 'Were you so sure that I should come?'

His brows rose a fraction, but his voice was friendly. 'I booked a table while you were changing.' He smiled a little then and went on: 'I'm famished—we had a scratch meal at midday, didn't we? We'll have a drink and decide what to order, shall we?'

She sipped her Dubonnet and studied the menu. There was a great deal to choose from and to her at least it was wildly expensive. She remembered the canteen at the hospital, where they all counted their money before they decided what to eat, and uncannily he read her thoughts. 'The food's pretty basic

118

at St Athel's, isn't it? What does it cost you to eat there?'

He asked the question with seeming idleness so that she was lulled into an unthinking answer. 'Well, I try to keep it down to three or four pounds a day, less if I can—we can't get pudding for that or any of the extras, but we all have tea and biscuits in our rooms, you know, and we share those round—and we buy chips.'

His expression didn't alter, only his eyes narrowed so that she was unable to read the expression in his face. She went on: 'Of course, we all eat too much starch, but it's nice and filling even though it's awfully bad for our figures.'

His voice was pleasantly detached. 'There doesn't seem much wrong with yours, dear girl,' and he twinkled at her so nicely that she chuckled.

'Well, I run round rather a lot, don't I?'

'You do—you work damned hard. I like your Mrs Mead, by the way. What a sensible woman she is—your right hand, I presume.'

The talk drifted to the shared interest of their work, and it was several minutes before he asked: 'Now, what shall we have? How about pâté for a start? We could follow it with salmon—they do it very nicely here with asparagus tips and quenelles of sole.'

Letitia wasn't at all sure what a quenelle was, but

it sounded nice. She agreed happily, disposed of the pâté when it came with real pleasure, and ate the salmon which followed it with an excellent appetite, and when she sipped the wine he had taken time in ordering, she said appropriately: 'Oh, claret, isn't it?'

He looked at her with some interest. 'How delightful to take out a girl who doesn't think only in terms of champagne and sherry. Where did you get your knowledge from? Do wines interest you?'

'I expect they would if I drank them more often,' she told him ingenuously. 'Father knows a lot about them and he says that everyone, women too, should have a knowledge of them, even if they never get a chance to drink anything else but the cooking sherry.'

'Your father is a most interesting man.'

She speared some salmon and popped it into her mouth. She had forgotten all about being awkward and disliking men; she felt, for the first time in weeks, composed and assured. It was a delightful sensation, and went, like the excellent claret, to her head just a little, so that she talked happily through the delicious trifle which arrived after the salmon, and well into the coffee, quietly encouraged by her companion, who, while not saying much himself, asked the right questions in the right places and looked interested. They sat a long time over their leisurely meal, and when at length he drove her back to St Athel's, she thanked him fervently for her evening.

Jason had got out of the BMW too, and they stood facing each other under the bright lights of the Accident Room entrance. She looked up at him, glowing with her love so that her cheeks were prettily pink and her eyes shone, and he stared back.

'Well, dear girl, that wasn't such an ordeal, was it?' he asked. 'For a nice girl who isn't so very plain, you made a great success of our evening.' His smile robbed the words of any unkindness. 'Looks don't count in the long run, you know, Letitia, but charm does, and you have plenty of that—and mind you remember it. I dare say Karel asked you to go out with him?' His voice had lost none of its calm, and when she nodded: 'He's a good chap—you'll enjoy yourself with him.'

The happy glow faded; this then was why he had taken her out—not so much for the pleasure of her company but to prove to her that she didn't need to worry about being dull or plain; that she could be an amusing companion for any young man who chose to ask her out—to break as it were the ice she had embeded herself in. A kindly act, but had he not, all along, begged her to consider him as an uncle? And now he had offered her avuncular advice!

She opened her eyes wide to hold back the tears,

and managed to smile. 'I'll take your advice, Jason.
It was a lovely evening.' She offered a hand and had
it gently engulfed. 'I hope you have a good trip to
Holland, and please give my love to Katrina.'

He was still holding her hand. 'Oh, lord, I quite
forgot that I was going to talk to you about her.
Never mind, Margo has it more or less fixed up.'

She had no idea what he was talking about and
when she asked all he said was: 'She'll tell you.
Good night, dear girl,' and he didn't kiss her, though
she had hoped that he would. She wished him good
night too in a sober little voice, then went through
the door he was holding open for her and ran across
the bare, deserted expanse of the Accident Room
and into the passage beyond without looking back.
She made herself think of nothing at all while she
got ready for bed, but the moment the light was out
she was powerless to prevent her thoughts flooding
back, and after a little while she allowed them to
take over, lying with her eyes tight shut in the hope
that sleep would come. It was a long while before
it did, so that when she went on duty the next morning she looked washed out and her eyes felt like hot
coals in her head.

It was on her way to the canteen that she met
Margo, who stopped her with a sisterly: 'Tishy,
whatever is the matter? You look absolutely grim!'
And after a long look. 'Have you got a cold?'

Letitia shook her head, admitting vaguely to feeling tired.

'Well, it's a good thing you've got that holiday next week, isn't it? Katrina's bursting with excitement.' She paused and looked even more narrowly at Letitia. 'You do know she's going home to stay for a week or two?'

'No.' The surge of excitement made it impossible to say more.

'Jason was going to tell you—haven't you seen him since we were at Dalmers Place?'

Letitia nodded. 'Yes, last night.' She added: 'He said he'd forgotten to tell me something, but he'd leave it to you—I didn't think it was anything much.'

Margo looked a little amused. 'Katrina had never been anywhere else in England but London and Dalmers Place, so she wheedled Jason into asking me if I'd ask Mother to invite her to stay—you see, she rather took to you, Tishy, and she wants to meet Paula. So I telephoned Mother and of course she loved the idea—you know how lost she feels with only Paula at home. He's driving her down before he goes back to Holland. She'll be there when you go on holiday.'

'Yes.' Did that mean that she would see him again? she wondered. 'How long is she going to stay?'

Margo shrugged. 'I've no idea, but you'll be home for a week, won't you—and Paula will be there—they're just about the same age. If they get on well, I daresay Paula will be invited back. Nice for her.'

'Lovely. I think I'd better go to the canteen...'

Her elder sister looked her over with affection. 'Enough money for a good meal?' she wanted to know.

Letitia nodded; food would choke her, there was far too much on her mind. She would go over to the home and make tea. She had drunk one cup of this calming beverage when she was called to the telephone.

'A man!' shrieked a voice up the stairs, and Letitia, her head stuffed full with Jason still, tore down to the ground floor, her shoes and cap off, intent on getting there before he should become impatient and ring off. Only it wasn't Jason, it was Karel.

'Dinner?' asked his cheerful voice at the other end of the wire, 'and how about dancing afterwards?' And was she free that very evening?

She said yes without pausing much to think about it. Karel was fun to be with and perhaps an evening out with him would shake her out of this silly self-pitying state she had got into. On her way back to her room she wondered idly why he had asked her; certainly not because he fancied her, of that she was

quite sure. They were very good friends, but that
was all. Probably he wanted to tell her all about his
blonde friend; even more likely, he had quarrelled
with that young lady and was intent on making her
jealous by taking Letitia out for the evening, something he could safely do since neither of them were
emotionally involved. She drank her cooling tea and
began to tidy her hair; she was adjusting her cap just
so when a voice screamed up the stairs once more,
begging her to go down to the telephone for a second time and adding a rider to the effect that it was
a man again and would it be a good idea if Tishy
had a telephone installed in her room so that the
speaker might be saved the trouble of taking her
calls.

She ran downstairs, making her excuses as she
went, sure with childish faith that this time it would
be Jason. It was. His voice, calm and friendly, sent
a tingle of delight through her and took her breath,
so that her hullo was gruff.

'Ah, dear girl, I'm at your home with Katrina—I
expect you know about that by now.'

'Yes.'

'I intended driving back straight away, but your
mother's offer of lunch has made me change my
mind. I shall come up to London this evening and
cross over tonight. Will you be free after tea?'

The tingle turned to a warm glow; he must like

her just a little, if he was going to ask her out; even as she thought it she remembered she had just accepted Karel's invitation. She said in a small voice: 'I'm going out with Karel.'

'You'll enjoy that.' His voice, though she strained her ear to catch any change in its tone, sounded as placid as it always did; she wondered if he had put Karel up to it in the first place, and the idea made her add snappishly: 'Yes, I shall—he's such fun.' And then, because her feelings were threatening to overcome her: 'I really must go, I'm on duty in five minutes.'

'Of course, dear girl. Any messages for your mother?'

'Please give her my love. I hope you have a pleasant trip home.'

There was no tinge of regret in his good-bye, so Letitia hung up and tore upstairs to her room to put on her shoes and emerge a few seconds later, looking neat and tidy and unnaturally prim—a magnificent effort on her part when what she really wanted to do was to fling herself on to her bed and howl her eyes out.

There was no time to indulge in such weak feelings, however. She was kept hard at work until she went off duty, and the serious business of making the best of herself for Karel's benefit took all her attention then—a waste of time and effort, it turned out, for although he was pleased to see her and took her to one of the trendier restaurants for dinner, it was obvious that his pleasure in her company was largely due to the fact that she made a sympathetic audience while he alternately sang the praises of the blonde and then, sunk in the depths of despair because of their recent quarrel, begged Letitia for advice.

And when they danced presently, he kept up a monologue in her ear, recalling how he and his blonde had danced together, and how wonderful a dancer she was, so that Letitia felt she had two left feet and ought not to be on the floor at all. All the same, Karel was a dear, and once he was on good terms with his girlfriend once more, or had found himself another one altogether, he would be quite his old self. As it was, he had spared no expense on their evening and when he took her back to the hospital, told her that she was a jolly good sort and kissed her in a brotherly fashion, observing that she was a nice girl, and she, heartily sick of his tepid compliment, thanked him with charm, wished him luck with his blonde and took herself off to her room, where she got ready for bed and presently, lying in the dark, indulged at last her overwhelming wish to have a good cry.

The week before her holidays went surprisingly fast; for one thing, they were busy in theatre, so that much of her free time was taken up with getting her clothes ready, and for another, Georgina came up to do some shopping and invited her to join her and Margo for tea at Fortnum and Mason, luckily on an afternoon when she was free, for she liked the elegant tea room and hoped that someone, during the afternoon, would mention Jason. No one did, though there was plenty of talk about Katrina's visit. 'A nice child,' said Georgina. 'You would think that being the youngest of such a large family she would be spoilt, but she isn't—she's clever, of course—they all are. That family has everything although none of them ever mentions it.' She smiled at Letitia, listening avidly. 'Have another of these little cakes, Tishy, I'm going to; I shouldn't really, for I might get fat and Julius will tease me.'

Julius wouldn't do anything of the sort, thought Letitia; he would love Georgina whatever shape she was; probably he thought she was the most beautiful girl in the world. She sighed, wishing with all her heart that she might be loved like that. By Jason, of course.

She went home by train, with Margo to see her off at Paddington and the promise of her father to meet her at Exeter. The train was full and hot and she slept uneasily, waking finally just before they reached Exeter. It was nice to see her father waiting on the platform, she hugged him with delight and got into the car beside him and they drove through the busy city streets and out on to the Moretonhampstead road, and as they left the city behind them she felt the breeze blowing coolly through the car windows. 'This is glorious,' she told her father, and he smiled understandingly. 'It's splendid to have you home, Tishy,' he told her fondly, 'although a week isn't long enough. That nice child Katrina seems to be enjoying herself, she and Paula get on very well together, but she's looking forward to seeing you again. Jason brought her down, of course— a splendid man; knows about porcelain, too. He much admired that Minton parian figure...'

'The dancer?'

Her father nodded. 'He's fortunate enough to have a pair—children with dogs. I imagine he has quite a collection of his own, I should dearly love to see it.' He sounded wistful, so that she said robustly: 'Yes, I daresay, Father, but you have some nice pieces yourself, you know—what about that Derby biscuit figure?'

Her parent brightened. 'A splendid example,' he agreed happily. 'Jason assured me that it was one of the best examples he had ever seen.'

Jason, it seemed, had impressed her father. He had impressed her too, though in a different way, but there was no point in thinking about that now, so she asked about her sisters and kept the conversation strictly on the family for the rest of their journey.

It was wonderful to be home, to be hugged and kissed by her mother, embraced joyfully by Paula and Katrina, and then borne away to eat a huge tea with everyone talking at once, making plans sufficient to last a month, let alone a week.

'What happened to the gipsies?' asked Letitia.

Her father sighed. 'They made a splendid recovery and discharged themselves two days ago. They're back in their usual haunt and the boy came to fetch his dog only this morning.'

'But it's too soon.'

'Yes, Tishy, by our standards it is, but not from theirs. Probably they'll regain their strength twice as quickly as any of us soft-living people. They're children of Nature, you know.'

She registered a silent resolve to go and see them for herself; it would have to be when Katrina wasn't about though, she didn't think that Jason would want his young sister to go with her. Her mind made up on that score, she flung herself into the enthusiastic plans for the week ahead.

The good weather held. They were able to go somewhere everyday, walking on Dartmoor, driving down to Dartmouth and Salcombe, laden with the picnic basket and with Shep taking up much of the back seat. Letitia drove, with Katrina beside her and her parents wedged in the back, and once there, they bathed and lay about in the sun and ate hugely, coming home in time to get tea before Paula got back from school. It was delightful. Letitia, lulled by fresh air and the peace and leisure of the countryside, felt her touchy nerves soothed, and even though she wasn't happy, at least she was beginning to think sensibly. She could even listen to Katrina talking about Jason—something which she did very frequently—without her breath catching in her throat and her heart turning over. She assured herself that given time, she would be able to forget him; she had got over Mike, now she would get over Jason— sentiments which did her credit and held no water at all. Jason wasn't Mike; he wasn't just any man, she would never be able to forget him. All the same, she tried hard and by the Saturday morning, with only one day to go before she had to return to St Athel's, she considered that she was well on the way to relegate him into his proper place in her life—a casual acquaintance whom it had been pleasant to meet but who could just as casually be forgotten. She assured herself of this fact repeatedly, with absolutely no success, although she reminded herself that it was early days yet.

Paula and Katrina were going over to the doctor's house to play tennis after breakfast, which left Letitia free at last to visit the gipsies. She got up early, dressed without much thought as to her appearance in slacks and a denim shirt, and went downstairs to get breakfast. She had it ready by the time everyone else came down, and the moment the girls had gone she whisked through the chores, told her mother vaguely that she was going for a walk, and set off.

She was glad to reach the trees, for the sun was already hot on her shoulders, and once in their shelter she didn't hurry, but poked around her as she went there was plenty to see; wild flowers of all kinds, a multitude of birds and the wood's four-footed inhabitants. She whistled to the birds as she strolled along the path, then stood patiently waiting for them to reply, so that it took her some time to reach the path which would lead her to where the gipsies were camped in the clearing. She turned down it, still not hurrying; the girls wouldn't be home for lunch, her mother wouldn't mind if she got home late; it would be cold meat and a salad and she could help herself from the huge, old-fashioned larder. She paused to watch a blackbird, and when it flew away whistled to it. The answering whistle wasn't one that any ornithologist would mistake for a genuine bird call, and Letitia turned round to see who it was. Jason, coming towards her.

He came without haste and nor did he appear eager, just his usual calm self, and she wondered crossly if he ever allowed any deep emotion to disturb him. He certainly wasn't displaying his feelings now, if he had any. His: 'Hullo, dear girl,' was uttered in a voice which, while friendly, held nothing more.

She stayed quietly, waiting for him to catch up with her and said in her turn: 'Hullo. Have you come to see Katrina? She's playing tennis at Doctor Gibbs, didn't Mother tell you?'

He halted beside her. 'Yes, but time enough to see her presently. Are you on your way to visit the gipsies, by any chance? Your mother said you had gone for a walk.'

They were making their way down the path, close together because it was so narrow. 'Yes, they're back—did you know? They discharged themselves and I wanted to see how they were getting on. It was too soon.'

He said almost the same as her father had done. 'For us it might have been—they live nearer to Nature than we do.'

'Have you come to take Katrina home?' She had been longing to ask that, and now it had popped out.

'Yes, your mother has asked me to spend the night here and go back tomorrow. I'll give you a lift as far as the hospital, if you like.'

'Thank you. Are you going back to your home?'

'Yes—and staying there for quite some time, I hope. Katrina has visits to pay before she goes back

to school and my mother will be back from visiting
my sisters.'

She stopped to look at him. 'Oh—your mother?
You've never mentioned her...' She went pink then
because there had never been any reason why he
should have done so, but he didn't appear to notice
her discomfiture.

'She lives a few miles away from me,' he told
her. 'We get on very well. My father died three
years ago—he was a doctor too.'

'I'm sorry. Your mother must be glad that she has
so many of you.'

'We like to think so. As a family we get on very
well—just as your family does.'

They had come to the end of the path and there
were the caravans once more, with the horses by the
water and the lurcher lying in a patch of sunlight
between the trees. He got to his feet the moment he
saw them, his ferocious back changing to a pleased
whine when he saw who it was. His welcome was
boisterous, and Letitia, freed at last from his atten-
tions, made a few ineffective attempts to brush down
her slacks and was deeply vexed when Jason remarked: 'Oh, leave it, dear girl, they surely can't be
worth all that attention.' His amused eye swept over
her so that she frowned quite fiercely. 'Only a fool
would come down here in anything else but jeans
and a shirt,' and she was even more angry when he

answered: 'I take it you keep an unending supply handy?'

He had laughed gently as he spoke. Letitia scowled at him and then had to change the scowl to a smile because the gipsy woman was coming towards them. She was followed by the rest of them, the old man and the boy and the young man, looking thinner and paler than they would normally be, but their eyes were bright and they seemed surprisingly fit. It didn't seem possible that they could be capable of taking up their old life so soon after being ill. 'Do you really feel all right?' she wanted to know of the woman. 'Shouldn't you have stayed a little longer in hospital?'

The woman shrugged. 'But why, missy? It is not our kind of life, closed up between walls, and Jerry here, he missed his dog. We shall do very well. You'll drink a cup of tea with us? We're beholden to you both for your help—you and the kind gentleman here, and it won't be forgotten.'

She made an inviting gesture towards one of the caravans and Letitia, with a glance at Jason, started to walk towards it. She didn't quite fancy tea, but she was too kindhearted to refuse hospitality when it was offered. They sat on an old bench outside the caravan, talking to the men—at least Jason did; Letitia got up after a minute or two and strolled across the grass with Jerry and the dog to give some sugar lumps to the horses, and when the tea came, she sat down on the caravan steps and drank it with the dog pressed close to her, hopeful that there might be more biscuits in her pocket, and the gipsy woman sat beside her.

She had, from time to time, stopped to talk to the gipsies when she had met them, but never for such a length of time as this. They were no fools, she quickly discovered, and it amused her to see Jason deep in conversation about trout fishing and obviously enjoying himself. It was when she refused a second cup of tea that the woman offered to tell her fortune for her. 'Turn the cup three times, dearie,' she advised Letitia, 'and hold it upside down with your left hand.'

'I don't think...' began Letitia, and caught Jason's eye; he was still talking about trout, but he was listening to her too. She did as she had been told and the gipsy took the cup from her and fell to studying it.

'A tall, fair man, dearie,' she began, and Letitia saw that the men were all listening now. 'Trouble and strife, but the life of a princess is waiting for you, for I see wealth and jewels and great happiness. Just as it should be for a kind young lady like you are.'

Her dark eyes flickered over Letitia's face. 'You don't believe me, but mark my words, missy, I'm one to tell the truth and that's what I see in the tea-leaves.' She cast the cup away from her and turned to Jason. 'And you, kind gentleman, shall I tell you your fortune?'

He answered her gravely: 'There is no need, I think,' and the woman nodded back at him.

'You're right, there is no need; I've told it all.' A remark of which Letitia took little notice; it had been easy enough for the gipsy to talk about a tall fair man when there was one standing beside her, and one was always told about the money and jewels and happiness waiting to brighten one's future. She didn't believe a word of it, although she thanked the woman nicely as they prepared to go.

They were half-way up the hill before she said: 'I'm glad they're all right.'

Her companion tucked a hand under her elbow and because there wasn't much room, pulled her closer. 'You're a nice girl,' he remarked, 'though I believe I've said that before.'

'Yes, you have!' she sounded quite savage. 'I'm sick and tired of being called nice—everyone says it!' She kicked at some nettles and when a briar tore her slacks she couldn't have cared less.

'Ah, yes—a bit monotonous, dear girl, but actually a compliment. A nice girl, from a man's point of view at least, means one who is pleasant to have around, with a soft voice and gentle ways and no ideas about contradicting him each time he opens his mouth, a girl who doesn't expect compliments with every second breath, or imagines that just because he is a man he's wildly in love with her.'

'She sounds like a hopeless prig,' said Letitia coldly. They had come out on to the main track through the wood once more and had turned towards the rectory. Jason took his hand from her arm and flung an arm round her shoulders instead. 'No, Letitia, never that, and just you remember that next time someone calls you a nice girl.'

Especially the bit about imagining he was in love with her, she supposed sourly. Had that been a veiled hint? she wondered uneasily. Surely she hadn't given herself away to him? She tried to think back to their previous meetings and became instantly confused; it was a relief when he continued in an ordinary voice: 'Katrina has had a splendid time here, I can never be sufficiently grateful. As she is so much younger than the rest of us I sometimes wonder if she has enough young company.'

'Well, we loved having her and I know Mother and Father will always welcome her if she likes to come again. Mother misses us all, I think. I don't know what she'll do when Paula leaves home.'

'It is the same for my mother, but of course there will be grandchildren enough to keep her fully occupied.'

'Your sisters have children?'

'Oh, a mere handful as yet, but I daresay that between us we shall produce enough progeny to satisfy Mama.'

She didn't mean to ask, but: 'You too—you're going to be married?'

He paused to look down at her, a little smile tugging at the corners of his mouth. 'But of course, dear girl—we all come to it, you know. Can't you see me in the role of father to a succession of children?'

Letitia could, only too clearly; he would be a wonderful father. She speculated as to the girl whom he had chosen—that Wibecke someone or other, perhaps; it didn't bear thinking of.

They had left the trees behind them now and as they crossed the rough grass he began to talk about other things, trivalities which kept them occupied until they reached the rectory, where he was instantly claimed by the Rector. Going to bed that night, Letitia reflected that she had seen very little of him during the day; certainly he had made no attempt to seek her out, only he had come looking for that morning, and had that been so that he might tell her, in a casual way, that he was going to be married? It seemed very likely. She closed her eyes on the unhappy thought, and hardly slept at all.

CHAPTER SEVEN

THEY LEFT after lunch the next day, with a decidedly mopish Katrina sitting in the back, and Letitia, who felt that way herself, took great pains to make conversation, plodding in an uninspired way through such mundane topics as the weather, the charms of the countryside at that time of year, the amount of traffic on the road, and adding a few observations as to the kind of crossing they might expect, the prospects of fine weather in Holland and the pleasure of returning home. To all of which Katrina answered only briefly and Jason with a civility which she found so dampening that after a little while she too fell silent. It was, she felt, someone else's turn. It was disconcerting when Jason, apparently reading her thoughts, said: 'Katrina is silent because she is unhappy at leaving your home, but presently she will get over it, and I—I am silent because I find it pleasant to drive with you beside me, knowing that I don't need to talk; that you won't mind if you aren't the centre of interest.'

A speech which Letitia found to be unanswerable; he had made her sound like a chatty saint who hadn't bothered much about her appearance; it also had the effect of drying her up completely, so that they sat in silence for quite some distance.

'Perhaps I put that rather badly,' Jason said at length, 'but you see, I think of you as a friend and don't always bother to choose my words.' He made it worse by adding: 'Are you sulking?'

'No,' she said forcefully, 'I am not—I have no reason to sulk, have I, with compliments pouring down on me at such a fine rate!' She gave a small, indignant snort and stared ahead of her, aware that he had cast a lightning glance at her, but he didn't answer her, only after a minute or two suggested at his most placid that they might stop for tea.

'How about Shaftesbury?' he wanted to know. 'There must be a tea-room there.'

'Yes, there is,' said Letitia, mollified at the thought of tea. 'It's up by the walks...'

'Which walks?' asked Katrina. Apparently the idea of tea had cheered her up sufficiently for speech.

'Well, the town's on a hill, and there's a walk along the ramparts, there's a splendid view and sometimes local artists hang their paintings there, and you can look at them as you walk and buy one if you want to.'

Katrina rested her chin on the back of Letitia's seat, her voice wheedling. 'Jason, please may we go to these walks if we hurry a little over our tea, and if I see a picture I like, will you buy it for me, then I will keep it always for a remembrance.'

He agreed amiably to this suggestion, and now that Katrina was feeling more like her usual happy self, the conversation became quite lively, so that the time passed too quickly, at least from Letitia's point of view.

The tea-shop was of the olde-worlde persuasion and dispelled the last of Katrina's low spirits. They took their tea in one of its small, low-ceilinged rooms and then walked to the ramparts close by. Letitia hadn't exaggerated. The view was delightful and far-flung, the flowers bordering the walk were at their best, and sure enough, hung almost the whole length of the wall, were the paintings. Katrina skipped from one to the other, changing her mind every few seconds until Jason told her good-naturedly that there would be no time to buy any-thing at all if she didn't make up her mind then and there. Finally she picked on a small watercolour of the town and they went along to the end of the walk to where a woman was sitting at a table, knitting. Jason had paid her and Letitia was turning away when Katrina exclaimed: 'But Tishy must have a painting too—Jason, buy her one.'

It didn't sound right, put like that. Letitia was on the point of refusing on the grounds of not liking anything when Jason said blandly: 'But of course—

I've seen the very one, but it's to be a surprise. I'm going to get it now, but you're not to open it until you get back to the hospital.'

It would have been churlish to have refused. She thanked him nicely and strolled with Katrina to the end of the walk while he retraced his steps. He caught up with them as they reached the main street, the picture under his arm, and Letitia spent the rest of their journey consumed with curiosity as to what it might be. Only after they had reached St Athel's and they had wished each other good-bye, with almost tearful affection on Katrina's part and careless friendliness on her brother's, did Letitia climb the stairs to her room and once there, before unpacking or putting on the kettle for a cup of tea, open her package.

The picture was a watercolour; she had seen it as they had walked along the line of paintings that after noon—a gentle painting of a small stream under the trees, with gipsies and a caravan beside it, not quite the same as the other, live gipsies, but sufficiently like to recall them vividly. For no reason at all she felt tears prick her eyes so that she had to sniff violently and blow her nose. She laid the picture down carefully on her bed and went to put on the kettle in the pantry at the end of the corridor. She met several of her friends on the way, which meant a pooling of tea, sugar and milk and much searching in cupboards for food, and when the ever-increasing number of young ladies had crowded into her room and one, inevitably, remarked on the picture, Letitia was able to say quite cheerfully that she had had it as a present, and no one had wanted to know who from; she had just been home and was presumably a gift from her family.

When everyone had gone, she walked over to the hospital, to the engineer's room in the basement, begged a nail from him and hammered it in with the heel of one of her winter boots. They weren't really supposed to hang pictures in their rooms, but it was a rule which, over the years, had lapsed. It looked exactly right on the wall opposite her bed and it would be the first thing she saw when she woke each day.

There was a heavy list in the morning and by the end of the first hour Letitia felt as though she hadn't been away at all. The patients were fetched, anaesthetized, operated upon and handed over to her care with a speed which was too good to last. It was almost time for her to go to dinner when an elderly man, admitted as a casualty with a stab wound in the chest, collapsed a few minutes after she had received him from the scrub nurse. She went to work on him at once, calling to Mrs Mead to warn the theatre, so that Julius came immediately, wasting no words, but dealing with the crisis with silent speed, while Letitia, well versed in such urgent work, handed him instruments, turned cylinder taps on and off when he told her to, erected a second drip and took the patient's blood pressure, it gave faint results presently and Julius said quietly: 'Good—I think we've got him,' and gave her a long list of instructions which she filed away neatly inside her sensible head.

It was another hour before the man was fit to be transferred to the ITU, and by then dinner time had come and gone, and what was more, the afternoon list was looming. Letitia retired to the changing room and gobbled the sandwiches Mrs Mead had fetched for her, drank some scalding coffee and without stopping to do anything to her face or hair, got into her theatre dress again and bundled on the mob cap, and even though the afternoon held no surprises, she was very tired by the time the list was finished, and hungry too. But it was only five o'clock, there would be no supper for another two hours and she had nothing to eat in her room. She finished tidying the recovery room, poked her head round Theatre door to wish Sister good night, and went over to her room.

She would have to go out to eat; there was a cheap little café just down the road where she could get a meal. She had a bath and changed into a cotton dress, then counted her money; she hadn't a great deal, but egg and chips would do nicely and if she had a pot of tea and some bread and butter she wouldn't need to go to supper. She did her face and hair in a hurry and went quickly down the stairs and through the hospital to the front entrance. The Head Porter, Nathaniel, was just taking over door duty and saluted her in the fatherly fashion he used towards the younger nurses.

'Got a date, Staff?' he wanted to know.

'Who—me? Heavens, no. I missed my dinner and I can't wait for supper, Nathaniel. I'm going down to the Cosy Café for a meal.'

She grinned at him and waved and went on her way, out into the busy street, packed with people going home from work, and grey and grimy despite the sunshine. The café wasn't very full, and Fred, who owned it, greeted her with a friendly nod; over the years the nurses at St Athel's had patronized him, and he knew most of them by sight. He came over to her table at once, wiped its plastic top and moved the pepper and salt an inch or two. 'What'll it be, luv?' he wanted to know.

'Egg and chips, please, Fred, and some bread and butter and a pot of tea. I missed my dinner.'

'And that's a damned shame, ducks—won't keep yer a mo'.'

It was stuffy in the little place, its air laden with the smells of warm vinegar and fried food and washing up, but it was nice to sit down and anticipate her supper. When the tea came Letitia poured herself a cup and then began on the egg and chips, eating slowly to make them last, wondering if she would be extravagant and have another lot. She decided against it; she had to have new duty shoes before the end of the month, and it was Margo's birthday in a week's time, and she would need money for those. She sighed and nibbled a chip, telling herself that if she ate too much she might get fat; she became so engrossed in this possibility that she failed to hear the doorbell pinging as it was opened. Only when Jason sat down in the chair opposite hers did she look up to stare at him, her mouth, luckily empty of chips, half open. After a long moment she achieved a 'Well…' and smiled a little uncertainly because he was smiling his nice gentle smile even though he hadn't spoken. When he did it was to ask: 'Is that your tea or an early supper?'

'Well, I missed dinner—we got held up, and the canteen doesn't open until seven o'clock.'

He leaned forward to study her plate. 'Egg?' he raised his eyebrows, 'and chips? I'll join you if I may, dear girl.'

He didn't wait for her to answer but lifted a hand to Fred, who advanced to their table. 'Friend of yours, ducks?' he wanted to know.

Letitia smiled at him. 'Oh, yes, Fred. A doctor who works at St Athel's from time to time.'

Fred treated his new customer to a narrow scrutiny which the doctor bore with good-natured fortitude, before saying: 'OK, what'll it be, doc?'

'Egg—er—eggs and chips, I think, and tea.' He glanced over to Letitia's side of the table. 'That is tea?' His glance lingered on her empty plate. 'I can't eat alone. Letitia, could you manage another plateful and keep me company?'

'Yes, I could, thank you.' She answered promptly and with no beating around the bush.

'And fresh tea for us both, perhaps?' He sat back, quite at his ease, while Fred took away the used plates and probably as a concession to his customer's calling, wiped the table down with extra care. When he had gone, Letitia said: 'I thought you'd gone back to Holland—you said you were going last night.'

He looked at her with lazy blue eyes. 'So I did, but when we got to Dalmers Place, Georgina insisted on us staying the night, and I can't get a reservation until tomorrow.'

'Oh. How did you know I was here?'

'Nathaniel told me.' He smiled again and looked around him. The little place was filling rapidly with bus drivers and their mates, shabby down-at-heel men with the evening paper tucked under an arm, and the last of the shoppers stopping briefly for a cup of tea before going home to suburbia. 'You should have let Karel know you were free and asked him to take you out to dinner,' he observed mildly.

'Me?' she exclaimed. 'Heavens, no—supposing he had arranged to do something else with his evening.' She wasn't going to mention the blonde, after all, Karel had confided in her.

The tea came and she poured them each a cup and by the time she had done that, the eggs and chips had arrived, and since Jason began on his with every sign of enjoyment, she felt no need to conceal the fact that she was still hungry. She ate up her second helping with as much appetite as the first, polished off her share of the bread and butter and refilled their cups.

'Fred cooks very well,' she observed, not because she expected her companion to be interested in Fred's prowess in the kitchen, but because it was something to say. The doctor agreed with her readily, admirably concealing the fact that he had never in his life before been into a place like the Cosy Café, and that egg and chips, while a wholesome and sustaining dish, had little appeal for him, especially at six o'clock in the evening. He had, in fact, been looking forward to a quite different meal in a quite different place, with a bottle of wine and Letitia in her green dress sitting opposite him. As it was, he stirred his strong tea and smiled across the table at her, putting her completely at ease and allowing her to forget that the dress she was wearing was last year's and her appearance, while neat, was hardly breathtaking.

She offered him the sugar and asked: 'Did you want to see me about something?' and his answer was ready enough even if vague.

'Well, I needed to see someone and it seemed a good idea as I had this unexpected day. I shan't be coming over again for some time.'

Letitia digested this with a sinking heart, her eyes on her plate. So many times she had thought: 'This is the last time,' and now it really was. Even if Paula went to stay with Katrina, and she thought it very likely, there was little hope of her being included in the invitation.

'Mind if I smoke?' Jason's voice cut across her thoughts and when she said no, she didn't mind a bit, he lit his pipe and sat back, puffing gently at it while she finished her tea, then signalled to Fred, remarking: 'You're tired, aren't you, dear girl? I've got the car here, I'm going to take you for a gentle run—just for an hour or so—you can go to sleep if you want to.'

She choked back the yawn which threatened and said brightly: 'That's awfully nice of you to suggest it, but it's such a waste of your evening.'

'No, I like a quiet run now and then.' He added carelessly: 'I intended going anyway, if you like to come along...?'

Put like that it was apparent that he wasn't just making a polite suggestion. 'Well, if you're really going?' she said a little inanely, and got to her feet, praised her supper to Fred and wandered to the door, conscious that she felt nicely full and more than a little sleepy.

They walked back to the hospital, talking trivialities, and when he helped her into the BMW, Letitia allowed herself to sink back into its comfort as he turned the car into the evening traffic and presently, down to the river, to go at a leisurely pace along the Embankment to Chelsea and over Putney Bridge, and when she asked him where they were going, his answer was: 'Oh, follow our noses, don't you think, dear girl?' which naturally enough led them to Hampton and a pleasant side road alongside the river, but presently Jason left it and found his way to Cookham, and all the time he talked, a quiet flow of words which needed only the minimum of answers, indeed, thinking about it afterwards, she was quite unable to remember what he had talked about, only that it had been soothing and undemanding, and when he stopped outside a charming inn on the river bank and suggested that they had coffee, she agreed happily. After all, she wouldn't be seeing him again;

she might as well make the most of the evening. It was still warm and not late and they went through the inn and out on to the lawn beyond, where they had their coffee by the peace and quiet of the water.

'This isn't at all like Fred's,' observed Letitia. It struck her then that the doctor wasn't really an egg and chips man; perhaps he was still hungry, for he was very large. 'Did you have enough to eat?' she asked a little anxiously.

A muscle twitched faintly at the corner of the doctor's mouth. 'Indeed I did—I found it a very decent little café, too. I liked the way Fred made sure that I really was a friend and not just being a nuisance.'

'Oh, he's always been like that; we're allowed to go there in uniform, you know, and he's proud of that and it makes him feel responsible.'

Jason nodded. 'What happens to you when theatre closes down?'

'I'll be lent out to the wards, I expect—night duty, too. I shall't like that—you see, it will only be for a few weeks, so I shall have to stay in my own room, not move over to the night nurses' quarters, and that means I shan't sleep a wink. People try to be quiet, but someone always drops something or forgets and puts a radio on loud, and there you are, awake for the rest of the day.'

'No holidays left?'

'Yes, three weeks, but everyone wants holidays

now and I've just had a week and they're short on
the wards. At least, that's what the Number Seven
told me. If I had measles or something they'd manage very well without me.'

He laughed. 'So they would. Shall we go? You're
on early in the morning, I expect?'

They went back a different way, through quiet
stretches of road, their surroundings dim in the evening light. It was almost dark by the time they
reached the hospital and the streets were quiet, too
early for returning theatregoers, too late for anyone
with a home to go to after their day's work. Jason
drew up outside the main entrance of the hospital
and got out to open her door.

'Did you enjoy your nap?' he asked on a laugh.

Letitia had tried so hard to stay awake; not to miss
a moment of his company. She said, her voice stiff
with annoyance at herself: 'I'm so very sorry, I tried
to stay awake...' She stopped, aware that she hadn't
put it very well, and he laughed again.

'Would you have gone to sleep if Karel had been
driving?' he asked.

'No, for he would never have given me the
chance—you should have given me a poke.'

She wondered why he sighed as he put his arms
around her. 'This instead,' he told her, and kissed
her.

She was surprised, for she hadn't expected that.

She stared up at him, her emotions churning around inside her so that she really had no sense at all. Then she stretched on tiptoe and kissed him back, and then, when he did nothing about it, said in a hopeless voice: 'Oh, Jason, good-bye,' and fled through the door and across the entrance hall.

She reached her room without meeting anyone and began to undress, appalled at her behaviour, appalled too at the strength of her feelings when he had kissed her, but then no one had ever kissed her like that before; he had wiped out Mike's milk-and-water efforts for good and all. And it hadn't been fair, it had made her forget her good sense and she had made a fool of herself in consequence—and what a good thing, she told herself savagely, that she would never see him again.

She was brushing her hair with terrible ferocity when Angela put her head round the door with the offer of a cup of tea. 'My goodness, Tishy,' she declared, 'you look as though you've been to your own funeral!' and she wasn't far wrong, decided Letitia gloomily.

Theatre worked flat out for the next week; as many cases as possible had to be dealt with before it was closed, otherwise when it re-opened the waiting list would be unmanageable. It meant that everyone on the theatre staff had to work longer hours and extra hard, but Letitia didn't mind; it suited her mood to be so busy that she had almost no time to herself and no time, either, to think. She made the extra work an excuse for going to bed early and joining, only for the briefest time, the sessions of tea-drinking which were usual in the home, and on duty she did her work just as well as she usually did, only with a quietness which discouraged the others from the customary chatting whenever there was a moment.

It was Julius who cornered her at last, strolling into the recovery room when the list was over for the day. 'Busy afternoon,' he observed laconically. 'Thank heaven there's another holiday just around the corner—which reminds me; I have something to ask you. Georgina is annoyed with me for forgetting…if I can arrange it, would you consider coming to Holland with us? Nanny's going to her home while we're away and Georgina thought at first that she could manage Polly and Ivo at Bergenstijn, but on second thoughts she isn't so sure. She wants someone there so that if we wanted to go away for a few hours, or even a day, the whole household won't be disrupted, and it has to be someone she knows and trusts. She thought of you. We must emphasise that you aren't expected to take Nanny's place, only be willing to take over if and when Georgina is away or caught up in the small amount of entertaining we do. Don't decide at once, think about it for a day or two.' He had gone before she had time to frame a single word.

She went along to see Margo after supper, perching on her sister's bed and drinking a mug of tea while she repeated the doctor's astonishing request. 'And he didn't stop for an answer,' she ended. 'He said think about it.'

Margo looked at her thoughtfully. 'Tishy, I think I should go—after all, you'll only be put on night duty until theatre opens again, and you know how you hate that. Julius can arrange it, I'm sure, and Georgina likes you, so you can be sure you won't be overworked. I've been to Bergenstijn, remember, it's well staffed and beautifully run.'

'Is it anywhere near…I mean, is it in the country?' Letitia longed to ask if Jason lived anywhere nearby. If he did, she assured herself silently, she wouldn't go, but Margo's answer made that unnecessary.

'Oh, it's on its own, nothing else close by, only a village, and that's small. There's a swimming pool and a tennis court and a gorgeous garden with a pond—you'll love it. You've been looking a bit peaked, Tishy—that week at home wasn't enough, a change of scene might do you good. I daresay Karel will be there for part of the time, as well as Cor and Beatrix and Franz—I don't know about

Phena. You'll know everyone which will be nice, but do as you like, love.'

'I suppose I might as well.' It would be nice to see the country where Jason lived, even though his home was miles away from Bergenstijn, but at least it would be better than trying to imagine it, and Polly and baby Ivo would fill her days nicely; when she got back to St Athel's the theatre would be going harder than ever. She would have no time to brood, and a good thing too. 'I'll go,' she said, then drank the rest of her tea and went back to her own room. 'I hope I'm doing the right thing.'

A sentiment echoed by Julius, miles away at Dalmers Place, sitting opposite Georgina in their sitting room. 'If I weren't your devoted slave, my darling,' he pointed out, 'I should have flatly refused to have anything to do with it.'

Georgina looked suitably meek. 'Well, dear Julius, I hadn't meant to tell you yet, but I did mention to Jason that we were thinking of asking Tishy to come to Holland with us, and do you know what he said?' She beamed at her husband. 'He said: ''George, you're an angel, I've been racking my brains how to get the girl over to Holland.'' Don't you think that was nice?'

'I don't know about nice, my love. I think that whatever you did or do it will make no difference in the long run. If Jason is serious about Tishy, then nothing will alter his purpose in marrying her.'

'Now isn't that a comforting thought?' murmured Georgina.

Letitia didn't see Julius to speak to until just before the afternoon list on the following day, when he came into the recovery room.

'I've a letter for you from Georgina. I fancy she doesn't trust my powers of persuasion. I'll leave it in the duty room, shall I?'

Letitia laid the last of the airways neatly beside its fellows. 'Thank you, though I've made up my mind already. I'd like to come and help you with the babies, if you really think I can be of some use.'

'I'm sure of it, Tishy, and thank you. Georgina will be delighted. I'll let you know in a day or two what the arrangements will be.'

She nodded. 'What about Miss Phelps?' The Principal Nursing Officer and a bit of a dragon in a nice way.

'Leave her to me. As for clothes and so on, Georgina will telephone you.' A remark which set up a pleasant enough train of thought in Letitia's mind. Life would be quiet at Bergenstijn, but she would have to decide what to take of her rather meagre wardrobe; it kept her nicely occupied.

Georgina telephoned the next evening, just as Letitia was getting into the bath—indeed, she had actually got one foot in the water when there was a terrific thump on the door and a voice shrieked at her to go down to the telephone. She didn't wait to dry the foot but flung her dressing gown about her person and pattered down the stairs, leaving damp marks as she went. It was only as she picked up the receiver and heard Georgina's voice that she realized that she had been certain it would be Jason. Disappointment closed her throat as she said 'Hullo', but Georgina didn't seem to notice anything wrong; she plunged at once into plans: they were to travel in three days' time on the Harwich night ferry and would Tishy mind having Polly in her cabin? And what about clothes? Three weeks, she cautioned, it all depended on how long they would take over the theatre, but a fortnight at least. 'So don't bring too much,' she went on, 'just cotton dresses and slacks and a pretty dress for the evening. That lovely green thing you had on when you were here—everyone said how sweet it was—oh, and a mac. Julius said it was all right about your passport, but I thought I'd mention it...'

'I already had a passport,' Letitia assured her, and added diffidently: 'You really think I'll be useful if I come?'

'Yes, Tishy, I do—Polly likes you, so she won't mind not having Nanny and I won't mind leaving both of them with you.'

'Well, I'll do my best—I'm looking forward to it. I didn't expect another holiday quite as soon as this.'

Georgina laughed. 'You wait until you've had Polly for a few hours before you say that, Tishy! Now, everything's clear, isn't it? Julius will come and fetch you, we can have dinner and then drive to Harwich, OK?'

'OK.'

It was surprising how easily everything went; Miss Phelps didn't seem to mind in the least that Letitia wouldn't be available for night duty; she spoke rather loftily about helping those who needed help in an emergency especially when the person concerned was one of the hospital consultants, and Letitia wondered what on earth Julius could have said to her. And her parents, when she telephoned, sounded very calm about it all; it was her mother who wanted to know if she would be seeing anything of Jason, to which she could only reply that no, she imagined not. It was funny, when she considered the matter, that she had no idea where he lived. He had never mentioned it and neither had Katrina. She promised to send a card when she arrived and a letter each week, and her father gave her a message to pass on to Jason about some porcelain, despite Letitia's certainty that she wouldn't be seeing him.

It was a decidedly pleasant sensation to be wafted

away from St Athel's in Julius's Rolls; she was tired, for she had worked until four o'clock that afternoon, but Julius, talking pleasantly about nothing in particular, revived her flagging spirits and they soared still further at Georgina's warm welcome when they arrived. They ate their dinner without loss of time and got into the car once more, with Polly, in her nightie and dressing gown and fast asleep, on Letitia's lap and Ivo in his Moses basket, sleeping too. At Harwich there was no delay. Julius drove on board and then with Polly in his arms, the two girls behind with the Moses basket and a porter with the luggage, led his small party to their cabins.

And very nice too, decided Letitia, looking round her. Small it might be, but it had everything she could need, even a shower, and the little brass beds looked very inviting. She tucked Polly into hers, refused the offer of a drink, wished her friends good night, and got ready for bed. She had never been out of England before and it was all rather exciting; if she had been on her own she would have gone on deck and had a look round. Instead she contented herself with several peeps from the small window before getting into bed and turning out the light.

It seemed no time at all before the steward was calling her with tea and toast, and Polly, waking up too, demanded to come into her bed and share it with her. They were making short work of it between them when Georgina came in, sat down on the end of the bed and picked up a finger of toast to nibble. 'It's only six o'clock,' she stated as Polly climbed into her lap. 'Julius has arranged to leave the ship last so we can have breakfast before we go. Could you be ready in half an hour, do you think? I've fed Ivo, he's asleep again, bless him. Did you sleep well?'

'Like a top.' Letitia drank the rest of her tea. 'I'll start on Polly now, shall I?'

Breakfast was a cheerful meal, with Polly perched beside her father and Ivo still asleep in his basket. The boat had been full and took some time to empty itself while they ate their way though bacon and eggs and toast and marmalade. By the time they had finished, almost everyone had gone; they went down to the car then and drove off the ship and through the Customs, on to the road leading away from the Hoek. Holland, thought Letitia excitedly. She stared out of the window and felt a thrill, even though the scenery was prosaic enough; and yet the houses that bordered the road were different, neat and square, the windows shrouded in blindingly white curtains.

Presently they joined the motorway to Rotterdam and there were no more houses, only flat green fields, very pleasant in the early morning. Rotterdam, when they reached it, she didn't much care for; it was large and bustling and in the distance were the ugly outlines of the oil refineries. It was a relief to leave the crowded streets behind, and tear on towards Utrecht. But before they reached that city, Julius turned off the motorway into a quiet country road, winding through water meadows and small woods, with here and there a house or two. It was charming, and Letitia said so.

'I'm glad,' said Julius over his shoulder. 'We live half a mile further on, down a lane.'

Georgina turned to look at Letitia. 'Jason has a house a mile from us,' she offered in her soft voice. 'He works mostly in Utrecht, you know, that's where his consulting rooms are. I expect we'll see something of him.'

She turned away again and Letitia was glad she had. She wasn't sure what expression her face wore, but inside her there had been a kind of explosion, happiness and surprise and a kind of panic at the idea of seeing Jason once more. She sat very still, taking the deep breaths she had so often urged her patients to take when they were agitated—it made no difference at all, she felt as though she were about to explode, perhaps if she were to shut her eyes…but when she did, there was Jason beneath the lids, so she opened them again, just in time to see the iron gates which guarded Bergenstijn from the outside world.

CHAPTER EIGHT

THE HOUSE stood at the end of a straight drive, square and solid, its large windows aligned precisely about its massive front door. Letitia, ushered inside amidst a little chorus of welcome, looked around her with curiosity and then remembered to mind her manners in time to shake hands with the elderly man who had opened the door to them.

'Hans,' Julius enlightened her, 'our friend and steward—and he speaks English.'

Letitia smiled widely and murmured suitably, then with Polly toddling beside her, went with Georgina into what was referred to as the little room, although it seemed remarkably large to her, but then as far as she could see, the house was large—Dalmers Place was large too, but in quite a different way, with a great deal of panelling and any number of small rooms, odd stairs and narrow passages. Here, she guessed, there would be plenty of space, and she was right, for presently, with Polly safely in Julius's keeping and Ivo sleeping in his basket, Georgina took her round the house, ending with the nurseries, two rooms at the end of the wide back landing on the first floor. Her own room was between them, with a bathroom of its own and every comfort which she had ever dreamed of. Being nanny in the Effert household must be rather super; Letitia was quite astonished when Georgina apologized for putting her in Nanny's bedroom.

'But it's beautiful!' she exclaimed. 'I've never seen such a pretty room, and it's got everything anyone could possibly want—besides, I shall be close to Polly and Ivo. I like it.'

'Oh, good. Let's go down and have coffee, shall we? Then we can take the children in the garden until lunchtime. Polly sleeps in the afternoon and Ivo wakes up to be fed.'

Letitia went to take another look at the nursery. 'Then may I sit up here and write some letters after lunch—I can keep an eye on them at the same time.'

'You don't mind? Everyone will be coming before dinner—Karel will bring the children with him—we haven't heard from Phena yet, perhaps she won't be coming just yet.' They started down the staircase. 'We'll work out some sort of timetable over coffee, shall we?'

It seemed to Letitia that she was being given too much free time, and she said so. 'I shan't know what to do with myself,' she protested, not much liking the idea of having too much time to think, knowing that her thoughts were bound to be of Jason.

It was Julius who said easily: 'Don't worry on

that score, Tishy—have you forgotten that my young cousins will be here? I doubt if you get a minute to yourself.'

They arrived late in the afternoon, laughing and talking and hugging first Georgina and then Letitia, talking Dutch and English as the mood took them, rushing to the kitchen to see Hans and Lenie, the housekeeper, tossing Polly into the air and going to admire baby Ivo. Even the dogs, Flip and little Schippershond and Andersen, the Great Dane, came in for their share of the excitement; the old house was alive with sound. Letitia, undressing and bathing Polly while Georgina saw to Ivo, was interrupted by the steady stream of visitors to the nursery—it was obvious that Julius's young relations loved Georgina dearly, while he could do no wrong in their eyes. A happy family; the sight of them together was heartwarming, although it made her feel lonely too.

They went to bed early, for they had all had a long journey of one sort or the other; it wasn't until Letitia was curled up in bed, the door open so that she would hear the slightest sound from the children in the next room, that she allowed herself to think about Jason, so close and yet so very far away. She was bound to meet him. She was still trying to decide how she would behave towards him when she fell asleep.

She still hadn't decided by the time she was getting Polly ready for bed the following day—it had been a busy one, but pleasant, for everyone had given a hand with the children so that Letitia had found ample time to talk to Karel, ask Beatrix and Cor about school and listen to the more serious Franz outlining his hopes of being a great surgeon later on. She had found time for a swim in the pool at the end of the garden, and taken Polly to admire the waterlilies in the lake. A lovely day, she decided as she obligingly turned herself into a horse so that Polly might ride her across the nursery floor. Halfway across it, they rolled over together, giggling and squirming, while Polly tugged the pins out of Letitia's hair the better to use it as reins.

'Ouch!' said Letitia, and rolled over to escape the small hands, narrowly missing a pair of large feet, expensively shod. Jason. She lifted a startled face to meet his amused eyes and felt Polly plucked from her shoulders, then with the moppet tucked under one arm, he swung her to her feet too, rather as though she had been a rag doll.

She was breathless, and not only because she had been romping with Polly. 'Bedtime games,' she managed. 'I'm a horse.'

He set Polly on a broad shoulder. 'You look like a girl to me. I asked where you were and was told that you were putting this moppet to bed—I imagined you going about your duties with no thought of horse riding, and what do I find? You, dear girl, looking every bit as old as Polly.'

'Well, really!' She was struggling with her hair and trying to look dignified. She hadn't imagined meeting him again like this; vague ideas of seeing him across a dinner table, with her in the green dress, looking serene, or failing that, coming— gracefully, of course—down the staircase with Jason looking up at her from the hall below. She frowned; things never turned out as she wished them to. 'Little children like a bedtime romp,' she pointed out coldly. 'Polly is going to have her supper now, and then I shall put her to bed.'

'No, Letitia, I shall give the brat her supper while you go and tidy yourself. Georgina will come and tuck her up as she always does, and the entire family will watch over both your charges while you, I hope, spend the evening with me.'

'Why?'

He chuckled. 'Shall we say that Georgina is concerned because you have had the children for most of the day and she thinks you should have a little time in which to enjoy yourself. You do enjoy yourself with me, dear girl?' His voice was blandly inquiring.

'Yes, thank you. But I came here to help with the babies...'

'Listen, Letitia, you're hardly expected to sit and brood over them once they're asleep—and anyway, the house is full of people.' He smiled with such charm that she found herself smiling back. 'That's better. Fetch the hot mash or whatever revolting mess this infant eats, and I'll stuff it into her. I told Georgina we would be ten minutes, so leap to it, girl.'

Letitia, leapt, unheeding of her resolutions about being serene and cool.

Twenty minutes later, dressed in the green, her hair immaculate, her face nicely made up, Letitia presented herself once more in the nursery. Jason had fed his goddaughter the supper she had fetched, now he was lolling against the wall watching Julius tuck his small daughter in for the night. Georgina was there too, with Ivo over her shoulder, half asleep and hicupping after his feed. A domestic scene, and it had apparently struck Jason in the same light, for he greeted her with: 'Ah, here you are. I've done my stint, I'm merely filling in time watching the experts.'

'And very good practice it is for you too,' said Georgina firmly. 'Now away with you both!' She smiled at them in a motherly fashion and Julius said something in Dutch to Jason which made him laugh as he swept Letitia out of the door and down the stairs.

In the hall she hesitated. 'Where are we going?' she asked suspiciously. 'Do I look all right? It isn't anywhere grand?'

He turned her round slowly, his head on one side. 'You look charming, and where we're going isn't grand at all, at least I don't consider it so,' They called good night to the others as they went through the hall and out into the warm evening. There was an Iso Lele coupé parked on the sweep and Letitia paused so that she might have a good look. 'What a car!' she exclaimed. 'I'll feel like a million in it—is it yours?'

'Yes.' He stood half smiling, saying nothing more, and after a minute she said: 'Well, I like the BMW too.' And when he still didn't speak she got in when he invited her and settled herself in its comfort, although this was a waste of time as it turned out, for it was barely five minutes before he turned the car between two stone pillars, the gates between them wide open, and raced up the straight tree-lined drive. There was a wall at its end with a wide open archway in its centre. Without slackening speed, Jason drove through and pulled up with smooth exactness before a nail-studded door set in the side of what appeared to her to be a miniature castle. It was of red brick, with curved walls and a number of turrets, with a steep roof rising to gables at either end, and although the sweep before the door was large, Letitia glimpsed a high wall and water to one side of it.

'Whatever is this?' she wanted to know as Jason got out, opened her door and held out a hand.

'Niehof—my home.' He had tucked her hand under his arm and was walking her towards the door.

'Your home—it can't be!' She knew that sounded foolish as she spoke, and added even more foolishly: 'It's a castle.'

'Well, it began as a castle—I hope we've managed to give it a few mod cons since then.' He opened the door and propelled her, very gently, inside.

The hall was a little dim, but pleasantly so, with the black and white tiled floor which she had expected in such an old building. The walls were panelled in some dark wood, with brass sconces set between a great many paintings. There was a magnificent medallion cupboard against one wall and facing it, a painted chest, richly decorated. Letitia didn't know much about furniture, but her discerning eye could see that they were very old, beautifully cared for and probably very valuable. She would have lingered to study the strapwork on the ceiling and admire the gilt-bronze chandelier hanging from it, but she was urged towards a double door beyond the cupboard.

'Come and meet my mother,' Jason invited.

She tugged at the large hand holding her so firmly so that he stopped to look down at her. 'Now what dear girl?' he inquired blandly.

'You might have said...I had no idea...rushing me out like this without a word!' Her voice rose peevishly.

'I distinctly remember inviting you to spend the evening with me.'

'Yes, I know, but you didn't say where.'

'You don't wish to meet my mother?'

'Don't be ridiculous, of course I do.'

He bent suddenly and kissed her on her surprised mouth. 'Dear girl, correct me if I'm wrong, but is there any point in this conversation?'

He had the door open and was ushering her in through it before she could frame an answer which would have done justice to the occasion. The room was light and airy compared with the cool dimness of the hall, with a circular bay window at one side, and two french windows at one end. And here the ceiling was elaborately decorated with fruit and flowers and cherubs painted in delicate colours, and these same colours had been repeated in the furnishings—the curtains, carpet and chair covers— they all reflected the ceiling above them. The furniture was dark oak, polished with age and endless care, and everything seemed very large—and that, Letitia discovered, included the lady who had risen from a chair by the window and was advancing to meet them. An elderly lady, not far short of six feet tall and built to match, but so regal in her walk that her size seemed unimportant. She was flanked on either side by two hefty Alsatian dogs, who at Jason's low whistle trotted across the room to greet him.

'Ah, Mama,' exclaimed Jason pleasantly, 'may I introduce Miss Letitia Marsden to you—I don't need to say more than that, do I, for you already know a great deal about her.'

His mother smiled, softening her handsome features into motherliness as she extended a welcoming hand. 'Letitia,' she said in a surprisingly youthful voice, 'I have been looking forward to meeting you, for I have been told endless tales of you by Katrina. Come and sit down, my dear, and Jason shall get us all a drink.'

Letitia sat, aware of bitter disappointment because it was Katrina who had talked about her and not Jason, and her hostess went on: 'The child had such a delightful holiday with your parents. It was kind of them to invite her, and she has made a good friend in Paula, who I hope will visit us in a little while.' The charming voice ceased for a minute, and eyes as blue as her son's smiled into hers. 'Your mother and I have much in common,' she went on kindly, 'for we both have large families.' She accepted a glass from the doctor. 'I do not live here, you know, but with so many children to visit I stay with each of them for a week or two at a time and then go back to my own home. I lived here when my husband was alive, of course.'

'How could you bear to leave it?' asked Letitia, and wondered if she had sounded rude. Apparently not.

'When the children were quite small, I told Jason's father that if he were to die first, I wished to have a house of my own so that Jason, who inherited this place, would feel free to lead his own life, so I have a very pleasant house a mile or so away—far enough, in fact, for him to feel that he need not study my wishes about each and every small thing. It works very well.'

She smiled at her son, stretched out in an armchair facing them both, and turned back to Letitia. 'And you, my dear, you lead a busy life, I understand, and you are also a friend of Georgina?'

Letitia, recovered from her initial surprise and fortified by the excellent sherry, agreed to both remarks, adding the rider that Georgina was one of the nicest people she knew.

'Indeed, yes, and such a perfect wife for Julius; they are ideally suited.' The talk turned to the children and became general, with Jason saying very little, and once or twice when Letitia looked up and

caught his eye she found herself forcefully reminded
of his kiss in the hall; she went a little pink, remembering it, and saw him smile.

They dined in another splendid room, panelled
just as the hall was, and with a similar ceiling, and
here the furniture was of a later period; an oval table
of walnut, with Chippendale chairs and a long,
gracefully shaped sideboard. The meal was delicious
and served by an elderly man who reminded her of
Hans and was introduced as Jacobus; as old and
trusted a friend and steward as Hans, that was obvious. Letitia, sitting between the doctor and his
mother, wondered how many servants there were in
the house, and if it was difficult to get them in such
a rural area, and as though her hostess had read her
mind, she offered the information that as well as
Jacobus, Jason enjoyed the services of an excellent
cook and two maids besides, as well as a full time
gardener.

'Only because,' explained Jason, 'the people who
worked for my father married and either lived in the
house or settled close by, and now that their children
are grown, they take it for granted that they should
work here, taking over from their parents—a pleasant arrangement and an enviable one, I admit. Julius
is in like case; you see, there isn't a great deal of
work locally and few of them care to make the jour-

ney to Utrecht each day. Certainly they don't want to live there.'

They began to talk of other things, and Letitia, full of curiosity about the enchanting castle she was in, had to bottle up the question she was longing to ask. She might have asked them if she hadn't been uneasily aware that Jason guessed at her curiosity and was amused by it. She avoided his eye as much as possible for the rest of dinner, and afterwards, when they were having their coffee in the drawing room, she concentrated upon her hostess, answering him readily enough when he addressed her, but making no attempt to attract his attention.

Letitia had hoped that she might be taken on a tour of the house, but no one suggested it. The two rooms she had seen had whetted her appetite to see the remainder, but she was, after all, only a guest for an evening, and a not very intimate one at that. She studied the ceiling with its enchanting paintings whenever she had the opportunity, and tried to imagine what the rest of the house was like, and with a careful eye on the clock, made her excuses at the correct time, dogged by the memory of guests who had come to dinner with her parents and stayed for hours afterwards, while she and her mother fumed silently, thinking of the washing up which would have to be done before they could go to bed—not that Jason and his mother would need to do that. All the same, she made her farewells without lingering, thanked her hostess for a delightful evening, murmured suitably in reply to Mevrouw Mourik van Nie's hope that they would meet again, and walked to the door with Jason, who had shown a disappointing calm when she had suggested that she should leave, and over and above that, had made no effort to prolong her visit.

There was, of course, no reason why he should, her common sense told her, but common sense could be tiresome at times and held no comfort; nor did Jason's manner—detached and pleasant and nothing else. The unpleasant little doubt crept into Letitia's mind that perhaps he had asked her to his home as a kind of gesture; his share of entertaining her during her stay in Holland, a doubt which wasn't dispelled during the short journey back to Bergenstijn, for he talked about nothing in particular and never once hinted that they might meet again while she was there. As a consequence, she was unreasonably cross by the time they reached the house, although common sense again warned her that it was absurd to imagine, even for a moment, that just because he had kissed her—and very thoroughly too—and invited her to meet his mother and dine at his home, he was being anything more than commonly courteous.

She got out of the car with a falsely bright: 'Oh,

here we are already,' and flounced into the hall, just in time to come face to face with Karel, coming from the drawing room.

It suited her mood very well when he greeted her with a warm: 'Hi, darling Tish, what a desert of an evening without you,' which was the kind of nonsense she expected from him and which she quite rightly put down to youthful exuberance on his part. Normally she would have told him not to be so extravagant in his talk, but now she said in a voice as gay as his own: 'Then we'll have to make up for it some time, won't we?' She smiled at him with such overpowering pleasure as she spoke that he looked quite taken aback, for she didn't seem her usual sisterly self at all, but he liked her and not for the world would he have hurt her feelings—besides, he knew all about her and the Registrar, and Georgina had warned him to be kind.

'I'll take you up on that,' he declared, and caught her hands and whirled her round. 'We'll have an evening out.'

She declared 'Oh, lovely!' with rather more emphasis than was necessary, but that was only because Jason was still standing by the door, watching them. It annoyed her very much to see that he was smiling faintly, as though he were pleased. She let go of Karel's hand and went over to him.

'Thank you for my delightful evening, Jason.' She

smiled at him, though it was an effort. 'I loved your home,' she told him. 'It was so kind of you to let me see it, and I very much enjoyed meeting your mother.' She couldn't think of anything else to say after that; what she had said sounded a bit prosy, and Jason was being no help at all, standing there smiling as though he were amused at some joke of his own. She said a trifle sharply: 'Shall I let George or Julius know you're here?'

His brows rose gently and the smile widened so that she went red and said with a decided snap: 'How very silly of me—of course you have known Julius all you life, haven't you? I expect you use each other's homes as your own.'

'That's right.' His voice was silky. 'And we've known each other since we were in our prams, all of thirty-five years, and that is a long time before you were born, Letitia. No, don't worry about me, dear girl, I'll find Julius.'

He nodded affably at them both and strolled off across the hall and down the passage which led to Julius's study. Letitia waited until she heard the door shut behind him before speaking. 'I think I'll go to bed,' she declared, and stifled a quite convincing yawn. 'Such a lovely evening, but Polly will be awake early. Is George in the drawing room still?'

Karel nodded. 'I say, Tishy—remember that blonde I was telling you about?'

She paused on her way. 'Oh, yes, but I daresay you don't.'

He laughed, a cheerful bellow which surely penetrated the study door.

'You're right, I don't—what a wonderful sister you would have made for a chap, Tishy. There's a girl,' he paused and was suddenly serious, 'she's quiet and sweet and pretty, but not so's you'd notice—a bit like you, I suppose—prettier, of course. She doesn't care much for me—not yet. I wondered if you would meet her when you get back to London—I mean, if she sees you and you tell her you know me...'

Letitia forgot her own heartache and retraced her steps. 'Karel, of course I will. She sounds a dear and I'll do anything I can—I expect she heard tales about you from some of your more spectacular friends and it's made her uncertain. You want her to see your more serious side—isn't that it? And if a parson's daughter vouches for you...' She put her hands on his shoulders and reached up to kiss him in a sisterly fashion, unaware that Jason had come out of the study and was standing at the back of the hall, watching them. She didn't see him then, only after she had wished Karel good night and started for the drawing room once more, and as she could think of nothing to say, she remained silent, as did Jason, only he smiled again. 'Just as though he were

glad,' she muttered to herself as she entered the
drawing room, and Georgina, looking up from her
magazine, exclaimed: 'Why, Tishy, is anything the
matter? You look…'

'No, nothing at all. I've had a gorgeous evening.
I had no idea that Jason had such a grand home—a
castle, no less.'

Georgina studied her face. 'He's not a man to talk
about himself or his possessions,' she said quietly.
'He's nice, though, don't you agree?'

'Yes,' said Letitia, and thought what an inade-
quate answer that was, and because there was so
much she wanted to say and couldn't, she wandered
off to look at the portrait of an overpowering gentleman in a bag wig, thus missing the look of satisfaction on her companion's face.

'I think I'll go to bed, if you don't mind,' she said
presently, suddenly terrified that Georgina would
start to talk about Jason.

'Of course I don't mind, Tishy, and thank you for
being so sweet to Polly and Ivo. I thought we might
all have a day out tomorrow if the weather's fine;
we can take two cars and do some sightseeing. If I
have Ivo in his basket with us, perhaps you'd have
Polly with you in Karel's car. We could go down
the River Vecht—some friends of ours live along
there, but they're away—they won't mind a bit if

we park in their grounds and sit by the water for our lunch. Would you like that?'

'It sounds lovely—you're sure you wouldn't rather I stayed here with the babies? I'd be quite happy, you know; the gardens are so pretty.'

Georgina spoke warmly. 'That's sweet of you, Tishy—I'll take you up on that in a day or two. We have to go to Wassenaar to see Julius's aunt and uncle. They're sweet but elderly and I think the children might worry them a bit, so I'll leave them at home with you. But Great-Uncle Ivo, he's quite another kettle of fish—in his eighties and an absolute darling and adores Polly. He's dying to see little Ivo, that's really why he's coming. You'll like him, though he's a bit outspoken.'

Georgina got up and cast her magazine on the table beside her. 'I think I'll go and sit with Julius until he's finished his writing—he likes that, and so do I.'

They went out of the room together and parted at the foot of the staircase. There was no sign of Jason.

But even with him constantly in her thoughts, Letitia found it impossible not to enjoy herself the following day. Karel might be head over heels in love with this girl of his, but he was still an amusing companion. She sat behind him in the Porsche, rather cooped up, with Polly on her lap and Beatrix beside her while Franz sat in front. Cor had gone in the Rolls with the others after a fierce argument as to who should go with whom, quickly decided by Julius stating firmly that everyone would change places on the way back. It was a blindingly hot day and lunch was a protracted meal with everyone sitting at their ease by the river. After they had eaten everything in the picnic hamper, Julius and Georgina stayed with Polly, who was sleepy anyway, and the slumbering Ivo, while the others strolled off, and it wasn't long before the younger members of the party went ahead, leaving Karel and Letitia together.

'Now you can tell me all about this girl,' she urged him. 'What's her name?'

He was only too ready to comply with her request. 'Mary. Her father's a solicitor, she works in the Medical Secretary's office, a sort of filing clerk, I suppose you'd call her. She wanted to be a nurse, but she doesn't like to see people when they're ill, although she's very sorry for them, of course.' He shot Letitia a glance, defying her to comment upon this, but she wisely remained silent, merely looking sympathetic, which encouraged him to continue at some length. He had been talking for quite a time before she managed to suggest tactfully that they should return. He agreed readily enough and catching her arm in his, began, for the second time, to describe Mary's perfections. She was quite relieved when the picnic party came into view once more;

they were all there, waiting for them, and it was Julius who inquired: 'Had a nice walk?'

Letitia answered, aware that Karel was still up in the clouds with his Mary. 'Very nice, thanks—we got talking.' She smiled at Julius, who smiled back, but although Georgina smiled too, she looked a bit put out. Getting into the Porsche again, Letitia wondered why.

Everyone left the house after breakfast the next morning to make the journey to Wassenaar, leaving Letitia with the faithful Hans and the two babies. The day passed quickly enough, and if from time to time she entertained the hope that Jason might call, she tried to ignore it. She put the little ones to bed at their usual time, had a solitary dinner with Hans at his most attentive, making sure that she ate the delicious food he served her, and then went up to her room. She had no idea what time the others would be back and if she stayed downstairs she would feel impelled to keep running up to the nursery to make sure that the babies were asleep, so she sat in the day nursery, writing a letter home. She had almost finished it when the door opened and Jason walked in.

His 'Hullo,' was casual. 'No one home yet?' he asked. 'Have you enjoyed your day playing mother?'

Letitia closed her writing pad. 'Very much.

They're darling children, you know, and no trouble at all.'

He smiled then. 'You sound like Georgina. You had a good day out yesterday?'

He looked tired, she thought, and longed to ask him why; it was terrible to love someone so much and be unable to say the things you really wanted to say. 'Oh, lovely,' she answered brightly. 'It was so pretty by the river. We had a picnic on the bank in someone's grounds, a friend of Julius—I expect you know him too?' Jason nodded and she went on: 'It was gloriously hot too.'

'Too hot to explore the charming walk along the water?'

She answered without thinking. 'Oh, no—Karel took me, only we were so busy talking I didn't see nearly as much as I should have done.'

He was still smiling, but his face had grown very still; she thought for a long moment that he would never speak again; when he did it was in his usual placid voice. 'You can always go again—I'm sure Karel will be only too happy to take you.' He went to the door with an abruptness which surprised her. 'I must go home. Good night.'

Letitia stared at the closed door, puzzled, wondering why he had come and why he had left like that—the conversation had been harmless enough. She frowned and went back to her letter, mindful of the promise she had made herself that she would try not to think of him more than she could absolutely help.

She didn't see him for several days after that. It was Georgina who let fall the information that he was entertaining guests of Niehof, and later Julius told her that they had all been invited to an evening party there; all except herself, for someone had to keep an eye on Polly and Ivo—and after all, that was why she was there, wasn't it? Only Julius didn't put it like that.

'It's an opportunity for us all to go out together,' he explained. 'Usually that's difficult when Nanny's away, and it would have been out of the question now, only you are so luckily with us, Tishy. Jason thought it a splendid opportunity.'

So it was Jason who had suggested that she should stay home! In that case, even if she were asked, wild horses wouldn't drag her there. She agreed as to the excellence of the arrangement, her face and voice so wooden that Julius gave her a long, thoughtful look, frowning a little.

It was that same day that Great-Uncle Ivo arrived, driven in a motor-car—a Packard—which should have surely been a museum piece. Georgina whispered that the old gentleman went to great expense to keep it in running order and absolutely refused to exchange it for anything more modern. He was a determined old gentleman as well as being outspoken, she added, and Letitia could see that she was right.

Waiting on the fringe of the welcoming group she could see that here was a very old gentleman, bearing a marked resemblance to Julius, with a great deal of white hair and piercing blue eyes, greeting everyone in his own good time, and when he at length got to her, he looked her up and down before offering a hand for her to shake. 'Plain girl, aren't you?' he observed in a booming voice. 'Quite a taking face, though—a little like Georgina was before Julius married her—and look at her now, quite a beauty.' He chuckled. 'That's what comes of being happily married. You should try it, young woman.'

'Chance is a fine thing,' retorted Letitia with some asperity, and he burst out laughing.

'That's right, girl—you've plenty of spirit. I don't care for mealy-mouthed women myself. A dash of spirit lasts you all your life, and looks don't—remember that. And now I'll see my namesake.'

By the end of the day Letitia decided that she liked Great-Uncle Ivo; his tongue might be sharp and his manner somewhat dictatorial, but he loved his family and his manners were perfection despite his age. In the garden after tea, taking Polly to feed the ducks on the pond before bedtime, with Karel as escort, she ventured to ask about him.

'I can't remember him ever looking other than he does now,' Karel told her, 'and I simply can't imagine this family without him. I know Julius is the head of the family, but Great-Uncle Ivo is a kind of figurehead, if you see what I mean. I think we would all like him to go on living for ever, and unlike most people, we none of us need his money. There's none of that standing around waiting for him to die, if you see what I mean.'

'I suppose you're very rich,' Letitia observed idly.

'Yes, we are. Some ancestor made a pile in the West Indies and it's been taken care of ever since. Jason's a wealthy man too, though I believe the ancestor who started them on the road to riches was a bloodthirsty type who fought for William the Silent. Not that Jason's like that; as kind and generous as they come—can't think why he hasn't married; heaven knows there've been plenty of girls only too willing. No, he's the sort to marry some mouse of a girl because he's sorry for her.' He paused and then went on uncomfortably: 'I shouldn't have told you that, I suppose—about Jason being rich.'

'It doesn't matter, what difference could it possibly make? I'm not likely to meet him again once I'm back in England, and I don't gossip.'

'Lord, no,' he agreed warmly. 'I say, you haven't told anyone about Mary, have you?'

'Of course not. All the same, I think it's a pity

you don't tell Julius and Georgina.' She bent to pick up Polly so that she could throw the bread they had brought with them to the family of ducks paddling towards them.

'Well, I can't—not yet. They'd not take me seriously—they'd think she was just another girl, and she's not.'

Letitia felt a stab of envy for the absent Mary, then had to stifle hysterical laughter when he went on seriously: 'You see, Tishy, you wouldn't understand—you have to be in love to do that.'

She put Polly down. She was in love, but it hadn't made things very clear to her, in fact she had never been so muddled in all her life. She said quietly: 'Well, Karel, the thing is—I should imagine—to be quite sure—both of you, and when you are you can talk to Julius and he'll understand. After all, you're old enough to marry and you've just told me you've enough money to live on—besides, you're a good surgeon, Jason told me so. You'll be a success even if you didn't have a farthing of your own.'

'You are such a comforting kind of girl,' he assured her gratefully, and flung an arm round her shoulders as they walked back to the house, and Jason, standing at the open drawing room window with Georgina and Julius, saw that.

Georgina made off with Polly when they arrived, and Karel wandered off after a few words with Jason, and Julius went with him, leaving Letitia, who fidgeted round the room, trying to think of some excuse for going too.

'I wanted you to know that I'm sorry that you can't come this evening,' said Jason presently, 'but I know you understand.'

Letitia rearranged the cushions on the enormous sofa before replying; of course she understood; what should Jason Mourik van Nie, a rich man who lived in a castle which took away one's breath with its miniature grandeur, want with a girl he had once described as quite nice? 'Of course I understand. Besides, Jason, I think you overlook the fact that I came here to look after Polly and Ivo—I'm being paid for it, you know. I hardly expected to be treated as a guest. They're all wonderful to me as it is, but there's no need to think that I mind. I don't.'

He was lounging against one of the chairs, staring at her. 'You've quite got over the Medical Registrar, haven't you?' he asked to surprise her.

All the same she kept her voice steady. 'Yes, quite, thank you.'

'Perhaps there's someone else.' It was a statement, not a question, so that she found it difficult to answer. When she remained silent, he said: 'I hope so, Letitia.'

She began on the cushions once more, for she couldn't stand still listening to him talking like that, and when he crossed the room towards her she held one of them in front of her as if to ward him off. He actually had his hands on her shoulders when she said in an unhappy little voice: 'Oh, Jason, please don't—not again, I couldn't bear it!'

He dropped his hands at once and she saw him wince. 'I didn't mean...' she began—it was no good, she would have to tell him that she loved him and that it wasn't fair to kiss her; heaven knew what she might have said if he had allowed her to go on, but he didn't. He said quietly: 'My dear girl, you don't have to explain anything,' and went out of the room.

When everyone had gone and Letitia had pretended to eat her dinner under Hans's worried eye, she went up to her room and sat by the window, staring out into the darkening garden. She had tried during the evening to think what she could say to Jason, but she had had no success, and now she was tired to death with only one thought in her head; that she loved him very much, despite the fact that he had never given her any encouragement to do so. A nice cry would have been the thing, but she seemed beyond tears.

CHAPTER NINE

THE PARTY had been splendid, everyone told her the next morning. Letitia listened to their cheerful talk about it, treasuring every mention of Jason, then suggested that as Georgina had had a late night she might take the babies into the garden until lunch time, an offer willingly accepted. Letitia went to sit by the lake, with baby Ivo in his pram and Polly busy picking daisies so that they might make a daisy chain together. It was quiet there; she would have been quite happy to have gone back there after lunch, but Georgina insisted that she should accept Karel's offer to drive her into Utrecht so that she might do any shopping she wanted, and indeed, she had presents to choose for her family. With his help she found something to please everyone before he took her to tea at the Esplanade Restaurant, a large cheerful place in the heart of the city. It was during tea that she managed to ask with a casual air where the hospital was.

'Oh, if you mean the one where Jason works—that's the largest, you know, we'll go that way presently, and you can see for yourself. It's pretty up to date.'

He was as good as his word, parking for a few minutes in the hospital forecourt and pointing out the various departments. Letitia looked at them all carefully, imprinting them on her mind, so that later on, when she was back in England, she would be able to think of Jason working there. It was cold comfort but better than nothing.

The days flew by; there was always something to fill them and whenever possible Letitia was included in the various outings, and when she stayed behind with Polly and Ivo there was the faithful Hans to look after her. She told herself that she was a very lucky girl, living in such comfort and with so little to do. She had struck up quite a friendship with Great-Uncle Ivo, too—it was impossible not to like the old gentleman, even though at times he was quite outrageous; besides, he often spoke of Jason.

'Knew him as a boy,' he told her one afternoon when they were sitting in the garden together. 'Young limb, he was—always at the top of a tree or away fishing or out with the dogs. He's grown into a decent chap, don't you agree, girl?' He had stared into her face so that she pinkened, furious at herself for doing so. 'Um,' said her companion thoughtfully, and then: 'God bless my soul!'

She was to go back a few days ahead of the others; partly because Karel intended to leave then and was giving her a lift, and partly because although the theatre would be opened again the day after she returned, Julius wouldn't be working until the end of the week. The last few days came and she had seen nothing of Jason; he might just as well have been at the South Pole for all the difference it made, but there was to be a party on her last evening and although Georgina hadn't said that he would be there, Letitia hoped that he would be. But as it turned out, it was the day before that when he came. Letitia was spooning Polly's supper into her small pink mouth when he walked in, so quietly that she didn't hear him until he slid into a chair beside her at the nursery table.

'Hullo.' He sounded as though they had seen each other only an hour or so ago instead of days. 'You're going home tomorrow, Julius tells me.'

'Yes.'

'With Karel?'

'Yes.'

'I've a free afternoon tomorrow, so I wondered if you would like to come over and see the gardens, they're rather nice just now.'

'Thank you, I'd like that,' and then, anxious not to seem too eager for his company: 'But I'm not sure about tomorrow, I must ask George.'

'I already have and she said go ahead. She'll be home all day, anyway, and had intended asking you if you wanted to go anywhere on your own.'

'Well, then—yes, I'll come.' It had been weak of
her to say that; why not make some excuse and say
goodbye now? That would have been the sensible
thing to do, only she wasn't sensible any more. She
stuffed rusks and milk, mashed together into a horrid
pap, into Polly's willing mouth. 'Good girl,' she encouraged her, 'there's a banana for afters.'

'Revolting!' declared Jason. 'And she actually
seems to like it. I've brought her some chocolate.'

'One small piece,' Letitia warned him, 'before I
clean her teeth.'

He was unwrapping it while his goddaughter uttered cries of joy from a full mouth. 'You'll make
a pretty fierce mum,' he observed, and added: 'A
rather sweet one too.'

'I'll have to get married first.'

But he didn't answer her, only smiled and presently took a casual leave.

He called for her after lunch the following afternoon, relaxed and elegant, for all the world as
though he hadn't come straight from a heavy morning's work at the hospital. Letitia had spent a good
deal of thought on what to wear, rather in the mood
of someone going to the block and wishing to put
on a good show. She had decided at length on a
blue and white striped cotton dress, last year's, so
neither new nor as fashionable as she would have
wished, but it was cool and pleasing to the eye, and

she had tied her hair back with a matching ribbon and got out her best pair of sandals to put on her bare feet; she had bought them on a shopping trip with Georgina; they were blue too, canvas with a rope sole and really quite the latest thing.

Jason gave her an all-embracing glance, accorded her a cheerful hullo, then addressed himself to Georgina and Julius, lounging on the terrace, and standing there beside him, Letitia was conscious of doubt about the afternoon's outing. After all, he had no interest in her, not the kind she wanted, anyway. There was no need for him to put himself out. He had, after all, already done his share of entertaining her. She began, quite foolishly, to think of an excuse for not going. A sore throat? or a headache? No good, both he and Julius would at once examine her perfectly healthy tonsils and know it for an excuse, and a headache was too old a trick. And there was no more time to think of anything else, for he asked: 'Ready?' in a voice suggesting that she had kept him waiting, and urged her into the car. It was the BMW this time and she commented upon it.

'I quite thought you'd got rid of it,' she added.

'Lord no—I like a change, that's all.' He spoke laconically and after that they said very little on the short journey, but when they reached the archway again, she uttered an involuntary 'Oh, it's absolutely super!'

He agreed placidly and invited her to get out. 'My mother isn't here,' he told her. 'My eldest sister's children have taken the measles, and Mama has gone, full sail, to render all aid.'

She turned to look at him. 'You sound as though—as though you don't like children.'

She was conscious of his hand on her shoulder. 'On the contrary,' he assured her quietly. 'Come inside, it's far too nice a day to waste it indoors, but there is one room, I believe you would like to see.'

Letitia would have disputed that point; there was nothing she would have liked better than to stroll from room to room of the lovely old place and examine its treasures at her leisure, but she could hardly ask. She agreed politely and allowed herself to be led down a short passage at the back of the hall where he opened a panelled door.

'This is the oldest part of the house,' he explained. 'It was used as the solarium by the wife of the man who built it. Mother used it as her sitting room, just as all the ladies of the house did before her. It has been empty for a year or two now.'

It was a small apartment, wainscoted to the plastered ceiling, with long windows leading into the garden, an open fireplace with its log basket and irons, and a high-backed brocaded chair drawn up to its side, flanked by a lady's work-table, the blue of its faded silken bag matching the curtains. It was a delightful little room; Letitia ran a careful finger along the marquetry ornamenting the top of a small circular table in the centre of it and exclaimed on a little sigh: 'It's quite perfect. I can just imagine your mother, and all the other mothers before her, coming here for peace and quiet—she would have needed that now and again, I expect, with so many of you...' She was thinking aloud, forgetful of her companion for the moment. 'There would have been a great deal to do—children to see to and meals to plan and the house to run, and time to be with her husband—she would have wanted that too.'

She went to look out of the window and said dreamily: 'And such a lovely garden too.'

Jason opened one of the french windows, and without saying anything, gestured for her to pass through. 'There have always been roses here,' he told her, 'so that whoever was in the solarium would be able to see them and smell them too—there's a charming herb garden, too.'

They strolled down one path and up another, pausing to admire the lily pond and the formal Dutch garden with its neatly clipped box hedges, the flowers set so precisely that they might have been painted on canvas. Presently he suggested tea, and they went indoors, Letitia's head delightfully full of scents and flowers and a glimpse of a vast kitchen garden which in its way was just as beautiful as the flower beds. They used a small side door this time, which opened into a pleasant room with a wide balcony overlooking a lawn edged with trees, and here they had tea, with Letitia nervously pouring it from a Queen Anne silver teapot into Meissen cups so delicate she was afraid they would crack if she raised her voice.

She had worried about being alone with Jason; that she might feel awkward or shy, perhaps, but she was neither. He entertained her with a flow of talk which steadied her nerves nicely, so that when he suggested that she might like to go on to the balcony, she agreed readily. They stood side by side, leaning on its delicate wrought iron balustrade while he pointed out the distant summer house, the tiny stream which fed the pool at the end of the lawn, and Jaap the gardener, bending over the flower beds.

'He's been here for as long as I can remember,' Jason told her, 'he must be well into his eighties and works a full day still. It was suggested a little while ago that he should retire, but he was so upset that no one has dared mention it since.'

'I expect he loves his garden. Does he have any help?'

'Lord, yes, dear girl. He has a couple of lads whom he bullies unmercifully, though they take it like lambs.' He turned to look at her, and she noticed for the hundredth time how vividly blue his eyes were. 'Letitia, will you marry me?'

She was stunned into silence, goggling at him, her mouth agape, her eyes wide. 'Marry you?' she repeated, her voice high.

He nodded. 'That's right,' he agreed calmly, 'marry me.' He smiled a little and she waited, for surely he would tell her that he loved her, then it would be easy for her to tell him that she had loved him for weeks. But he said nothing at all, only looked at her, his eyes half closed against the sun, still smiling.

Not wanting to, she remembered what Karel had said—that Jason was the kind of man to marry some mouse of a girl out of pity. Somehow she kept her voice level and her face calm. 'It wouldn't do, Jason—I'm not the right person. You see, I'm not used to managing servants; we've only ever had old Mrs Barnes at home and she comes twice a week and does what she wants. I wouldn't know how to go about things, and they'd hate it, and after a little while you would too. And it's such a large house.'

'Just a house, dear girl, and my home—and everyone, down to the boy who does the odd jobs, likes you.' He bent down to fondle the two dogs sitting so quietly beside him. 'That's an excuse, isn't it, Letitia? You're not the girl to care one bit that I have rather a lot of money and everything that goes with it—you could manage an establishment twice the size of Niehof, and you know it. You're making excuses, dear girl.'

She had looked away because she wanted to cry and he mustn't see. She wondered what had decided him to ask her to marry him—probably an impulse born of his kindness, not love—he had been careful not to mention that.

'Yes,' she said in a small, well-controlled voice, 'I suppose I am.'

He stood up. 'Well, we'll forget the whole thing, shall we, dear girl?' And now his voice was as placid and cheerful as usual so that she had to take a quick look. He was watching her with eyes still half shut, so that she was unable to read their expression. 'We certainly mustn't let it spoil a beautiful friendship, must we?' He went on easily: 'Tell me, which way is Karel taking you home?'

'We're to go on the Ostend ferry, I believe. He'll drop me off at St Athel's.' Letitia heard her voice, sounding quite natural, answering him, and it was like listening to someone else speaking while her mind grappled with the fact that he had asked her to marry him—and she had refused when it was the dearest wish of her heart. Jason was speaking again.

'Ah, yes—quite easily done. He has only a couple more months to do, hasn't he? Has he any idea where he's going next? He's a good surgeon, Julius tells me, so presumably he'll specialize, and do well.'

She didn't want to talk about Karel, who didn't matter at all, but Jason seemed interested, and they had to talk about something, didn't they?

'Oh, yes—I think he will, and he's very keen to get on.'

'And young.' There was edge to Jason's voice which Letitia had never heard before. Probably he was irritated at their awkward little scene; she made haste to find a topic of conversation. The garden once more; she wore it threadbare, but Jason agreed pleasantly enough to her remarks, and presently the conversation was back again on safe ground; trees and shrubs and flower-beds, until he suggested that they should go.

'I hate to bring such a pleasant afternoon to an end,' he told her gently, 'but if you are to go to George's party, we should be going.'

He had become the genial host, thoughtful of his guest, and his impersonal good manners chilled her to the bone so that any wild ideas she had been turning over inside her unhappy head were most effectively damped. She accepted his suggestion in a colourless voice and sat silent beside him, composing a little speech to make to him later, when they would say good-bye.

Only it didn't turn out like that. True, he went

into the house with her and stayed for a drink, show-
ing none of the signs which a man whose offer of
marriage had just been refused might have been expected to exhibit. He was his usual good-humoured
self, and when he got up to Letitia, who had been
watching him, forgot every word of what she had
planned to say. Not that it mattered; how could she
have said it in a room full of people? How did you
tell a man that you loved him to distraction and then
ask him if he loved you with friends and relations
milling round, listening to every word?

Letitia shook hands, and his hand was cool and
firm and nothing more, and she thanked him for a
pleasant afternoon and murmured suitably when he
wished her a pleasant trip home. She watched him
go, sickened by the very idea of going back to St
Athel's and longing to rush after him and say so.
But what would be the good of that? And perhaps
it was fortunate that she hadn't had the chance to
say the things she had wanted to say—she would
have regretted it later, for he had never said that he
loved her. Indeed, now that she came to think about
it, he had changed the conversation so quickly that
she would scarcely have had the opportunity to
change her mind if she had wanted to. Perhaps he
had regretted the words the moment they were out
of his mouth and felt nothing but relief.

She saw the BMW shoot smoothly down the

drive, not listening to a word Great-Uncle Ivo was saying to her, so that she uttered replies at random, causing that old gentleman to look at her searchingly and bark:

'He'll be back, girl, he'll be back.' Which remark brought her to her senses more quickly than anything else could have done.

'No, he won't,' she told her companion in an empty voice. For a frightful moment she thought that she was going to disgrace herself by bursting into tears, but she choked them back. 'Do you suppose this glorious weather will last?' She asked the ridiculous question in a voice which didn't sound like hers at all.

'No,' said Great-Uncle Ivo, 'I don't.' He went on fiercely: 'You're a silly chit of a girl—Jason's a man in a thousand.'

'Oh, do you think I don't know that?' she almost wailed at him. 'Please don't let's talk about him!'

His old blue eyes surveyed her unhappy face. 'We were talking about the weather,' he said at once. 'We are having a glorious summer, though you probably don't agree with me, Letitia—and we each have our share of it. You have yours, my dear—a slice of summer.'

'A small slice of summer,' she corrected him, 'and it's finished. I'm going back tomorrow.'

'Ah, yes—with Karel. Such a dear boy.'

'It's kind of him to offer me a lift.'

As though he had heard his name, Karel crossed the room to them and a few minutes later Letitia was laughing and talking as though she hadn't a care in the world. It was difficult, especially when she remembered Jason's nonchalant wave of the hand as he went, but life had to go on, however awful she felt about it. She would have liked time to think, but Karel gave her none; he was demanding to know if she could be ready to leave by seven o'clock the next morning, and when Great-Uncle Ivo strolled away, he confided: 'I telephoned Mary, and she'll be in London—we'll get a few hours together. You don't mind?'

She summoned a smile. 'Of course I don't,' and she sighed without knowing it so that he asked her if she was tired. She shook her head, unable to tell him that the day had become endless now that Jason had gone.

It was pouring with rain in the morning; unexpected and suitable to her mood, but it was impossible to remain miserable in Karel's company; he was at his gayest and she did her best to match his mood, while a part of her mind thought of Jason.

It was, in a way, good to be back at work; Letitia flung herself into the well-known routine, telling herself that now she was away from Jason she would find it easier to forget him; only she couldn't, she went around with a sad little face, joining in the lighthearted chatter of her friends, denying vigorously that anything was wrong when Margo challenged her in a big-sisterly fashion to tell her what was upsetting her, and throwing herself wholeheartedly into the mild activities afforded by the thin purses of herself and her friends.

She went out with Karel too. On the first occasion she quickly discovered it was to receive a briefing for the next invitation, when Mary would be there too. She listened carefully while Karel regaled her with dinner at the Snooty Fox. 'You see,' he told her seriously, 'you're just the kind of girl to convince Mary.'

Letitia spooned ice cream. 'What of?'

'Well, you know…you're so…so…' He paused, and she supplied: 'Yes, I know—respectable,' and he nodded.

'You mean that if she meets me and I say I'm a friend of yours she'll be convinced that you're respectable too and not just fancying her?'

He closed his eyes and looked pained. 'Tishy, what a vulgar expression!' and opened them again to add: 'Yes, that's exactly it.'

'When's the great day?'

'Could you manage Wednesday evening? Do you think this place will do?'

She looked around her. 'Yes, it's marvellous, and anyway, I don't know anything about these super places. Only would it be a good idea to take her—us—to the sort of place where she might meet an uncle or a father or mother—do you know what I mean?'

He picked up her hand lying idle on the table and kissed it. 'Genius!' he exclaimed. 'Of course! The Connaught—Julius takes George there. What a clever girl you are, Tishy.'

She grinned at him. 'Oh, I know—only don't go doing silly things like kissing my hand, will you? Mary might not like it.'

She would have liked a new dress for the occasion, but if she were to go home for her next days off, she wouldn't be able to afford one. She put on the green once more, quite sick and tired of it, and went downstairs to where the taxi Karel had sent for her was waiting.

As she got into it, she thought how right she had been to refuse his offer to come and fetch her, deeming it wise for him to concentrate on his Mary.

The evening began splendidly. Mary was a nice girl. She would, Letitia saw at a glance, be just right for Karel; she had a pleasant voice, a charming manner and was, moreover, quietly pretty, and as well as that, Letitia fancied that she had some rather old-fashioned ideas which Julius and George would approve of. They got on splendidly together, and Karel, a little over-anxious to start with, relaxed as dinner proceeded. When they had had their coffee Letitia, mindful of his suggestion, gave it as her opinion that she should go back to hospital.

'I'm on duty at half past seven tomorrow,' she explained, 'and I know you won't mind. It's been a lovely evening, and I hope we shall see more of each other, Mary—it's been so nice to meet an old friend again—' she waved a hand in Karel's direction. 'You're getting more and more like Julius, Karel, I expect you'll end up just as well known and liked. Let me know how the thesis goes, won't you?'

Mary, who had heard of Julius, looked happy, and Karel beamed. 'I'll take you to a taxi,' he offered as Letitia shook hands with Mary and started for the door. Half-way there she stopped so suddenly that Karel, right behind her, had to put out a hand to steady her. Jason was sitting at a table just ahead of them. There was an elderly gentleman with him, and they had been in deep conversation, but Jason had looked up and seen her. She walked on, her legs strangely wobbly, and nodded stiffly as she drew level with them, she was aware that Jason had stood up and that Karel had seen him too and expected to stop, but without looking back she crossed the foyer to get her coat, opened her purse to get its ticket and turned to hand it to Karel, struggling to think of some excuse for her strange behaviour.

Only it wasn't Karel, it was Jason. He didn't say a word but took the ticket from her nerveless hand, fetched her coat and held it for her. She wondered why he looked so pleased with himself as she thanked him in a die-away voice.

'Don't let me keep you,' she begged in a wooden voice, and was affronted when he said cheerfully:

'Unfortunately, you can't—I'm dining with some-one who would hardly understand if I were to leave him between the soup and the fish.'

She walked away from him, although it needed all her will power to do so. 'I can't think where Karel has got to,' she said over her shoulder.

He caught up with her in a couple of strides. 'Gone back to his guest, I should imagine.' His voice was bland. 'I offered to see you to your taxi and he seemed only too pleased to get back to his table.'

She hurried to the entrance. 'How rude, how very rude!' she breathed furiously. 'I was his guest!'

They were on the pavement now and the doorman had gone to the kerb to get a cab. 'As chaperone, dear girl? I caught sight of you some time ago and I saw Karel's face when he was talking to the girl with you.' He grinned down at her. 'One of the best moments of my life,' he declared.

The taxi was waiting. Letitia said icily: 'How nice for you. I'll say good-bye.' She made to get into the taxi, but he put a large hand on its door. 'Say what you like, Letitia. We shall meet again very soon.'

'I don't want to see you, ever again.' She heard herself utter this whopping lie with utter dismay and wished at once to deny it, but she was in quite a nasty temper by now and no longer thinking very clearly.

Jason allowed her to enter and closed the door after her, and only when he had given her address and paid the driver did he say cheerfully: 'All the same, I'll be along, little Tishy.'

Letitia raged silently all the way to St Athel's, undressed in a tearing hurry and flung herself into bed, where she lay awake for hours, very unhappy because she had said all the wrong things, and also because he might take her at her word and never come near her again.

A needless worry, as it turned out; he was there the very next evening. Letitia had finished tidying the recovery room and was standing aimlessly in its centre when he came in, and although she had hoped, deep down inside her, that he would come, she hadn't expected him quite as soon as this, and certainly not at that hour when she was barely off duty. His hullo was friendly and her answering greeting was nothing better than a croak. He looked wonderful, she thought foolishly, standing there against the door, elegant and cool and remarkably satisfied with himself, and he shouldn't smile at her like that, it did something to her inside so that she couldn't think straight.

'I don't give in easily, dear girl,' he remarked mildly, 'even though it may appear so.'

She found her voice at that. 'Well, there has to be a first time for everything,' she told him shrilly, 'and now please go away, I'm busy.'

'You're off duty.' He was actually laughing at her. 'And why are you so cross, my darling girl?'

'I'm not, oh, Jason, I'm not!' She stamped a foot and said loudly, quite contradicting herself: 'I'm so furious—if only I knew how to gnash my teeth! I'm a mouse of a girl and you're sorry for me, just like Karel said, and I will not be pitied and patronized...'

He interrupted her quite ruthlessly: 'What utter rubbish!' He stared at her thoughtfully. 'Ah, I believe we have the crux of the matter—what did Karel say, my adorable Letitia?'

It all bubbled out in a breathless rush. 'That you had a robber baron for an ancestor but you weren't like him and that you could have married a dozen times, only you'd get c-caught by a mouse of a girl because you were sorry for her.' She paused for breath and opened her mouth to begin another tirade, only she burst into tears instead.

Jason's arms were very comforting—a little tight perhaps, but what was the pain of a few crushed ribs compared with the pleasure of being within their circle?

'Don't cry, my love,' he begged her. 'I have never considered you a mouse—indeed, you have reminded me of a very small dragon on various occasions. A mouse would never have coped with a bunch of spotty gipsies or an inquisitive bull.'

Letitia sniffed. There was something she had to know then and there. 'You asked me to marry you and then you seemed quite pleased because I said no.'

He let her go and put his hands in his pockets. 'Let us have a heart-to-heart talk,' he invited, 'and then I will ask you to marry me again.'

She took a step towards him. 'Oh...' She got no further; the door behind Jason had opened and Sister Hollins came in. The Theatre Superintendent was a youthful forty with a charming manner which concealed an efficient, slightly domineering nature, which was probably why she hadn't married. The younger, more flighty nurses had been heard to say that it wasn't for lack of trying. She gave Letitia a brisk smile and said in a voice to match: 'What, Staff, not gone yet? I'm sure everything is in perfect order. Run along now.'

Letitia didn't look at Jason. She said: 'Yes, Miss

Hollins,' in a meek voice which covered a multitude
of feelings, and slid away to change. As she went
she wondered how Jason would get away—he was
a splendid prize for Hollins and she had looked as
though she was expecting a nice cosy chat. She tore
off her mob cap and theatre dress and in hospital
uniform once more, started for the Nurses' Home.
She would bath and change her clothes and wait for
Jason. She laughed a little; he was going to ask her
to marry him, wasn't he? Suddenly the world had
become a wonderful place.

Letitia charged into the labyrinth of passages
which would get her to the Home, and had almost
reached the main corridor, half-way down which
was the little door leading to a short cut, when she
encountered Miss Page, and Office Sister and a mar-
tinet. Letitia skidded to a halt within inches of her,
murmured an apology and made to slip past, but
Miss Page had no intention of letting her go.

'Staff Nurse,' she observed awfully, 'why are you
running? Is there a fire? Is there haemorrhage? And
your hair is a disgrace—hanging in wisps, a most
regrettable sight. I'm sure I don't know what girls
are coming to!'

Letitia murmured again in a subdued way, almost
dancing with impatience, and forced herself to listen
meekly to a stern lecture. Only when Miss Page
paused for breath did she mutter something soothing

and tear off once more, uncaring of her superior's admonishing 'Staff Nurse!' as she turned into the short cut at last.

It was a sharp right-angled corner. She took it at speed, straight into Jason's arms. She felt them tighten round her with a strong sense of delight even as she said: 'However did you get here? What did you do with Sister Hollins?'

'Who is she?' asked Jason, and bent his head to kiss her.

'Jason—not here! Everyone goes this way—you can't...'

'Challenging me, my darling?' He kissed her again, in such a manner that she forgot where she was, and even if she had remembered, it wouldn't have mattered any more.

'And now we will have our little talk, darling Letitia.'

'Not here—Oh, Jason!' Two porters, wheeling an empty trolley briskly towards the corridor, went past, their eyes starting from their heads; a nurse, wrapped in the arms of a large, elegant gentleman was an unusual sight. They looked the other way when they encountered Jason's bland stare.

'Your room?' he suggested.

'You must be joking!'

'Then here. Now where were we, my darling dear?'

Letitia didn't care any more. She was possessed of a delicious sensation of not being responsible for her actions and not minding about it in the least. 'I met Sister Page,' she told him, slightly light-headed. 'Do I look very untidy?'

He was a man of monumental patience. 'No, my darling. Why do you ask?'

'Well, she said I did—she said my hair was a disgrace and I was a regrettable sight for a staff nurse.'

'Your hair is beautiful, so long and thick and straight; you are, in my opinion, quite the most charming sight in the whole world, and there is no need for her to fuss about you being a staff nurse any more. You will be my wife, fully occupied in running our home and bossing everyone around, and I daresay a bunch of tiresome brats as well.'

She was enchanted. 'They'll be the most wonderful children—only you haven't asked me to marry you yet; only that afternoon on the balcony, and you didn't say you loved me, so of course I couldn't say yes, could I?'

He said thoughtfully: 'I have tried so hard to decide when it was I first found that I loved you, dear girl. Perhaps when I saw you in that deplorable pair of slacks and old shirt, coming through the wood to meet me and not so much as a hullo, but a stream of words in which dogs and horses and gipsies were all muddled together. But I don't think I was sure, not then, and when I did know that you were the only girl in the whole world for me, Karel was there and I thought that it was he, and when you refused me in such a businesslike fashion, I felt sure it was. But I had to be quite sure, so I came over to see you, and there you were, a kind of invisible third at dinner with those two.' He grinned down at her. 'And your face when you saw me—oh, you contrived to make it severe, but you couldn't do anything about your eyes, my love.'

She stretched up and kissed him. 'Jason, I do love you.'

His eyes, very bright, smiled down at her. 'Then I shall propose…' he paused, 'but not, I think, for a minute or two.'

The purposeful feet they had both heard rounded the corner. Sister Page, primed for wrathful speech, fetched up in front of them, momentarily taken aback.

'Ah, Sister,' said Jason smoothly. 'Good evening, and how delightful that you should be the first one to hear our good news.'

She eyed him cautiously. 'Good evening, doctor. I want a word with Staff Nurse.'

'I see that you don't quite understand,' observed Jason, still smoothly. 'Staff Nurse and I are going to be married.'

For a moment Sister Page looked like the cat who had caught a mouse and had it taken away. She cast a reproachful look at Jason and a frustrated one at Letitia and rallied sufficiently to say: 'Well, I'm sure I wish you both happy.' She looked at them rather uncertainly. 'Is it a secret?' she asked.

Jason answered: 'No, please tell anyone you wish.' He smiled at her and she smiled suddenly at them both before she rustled away, her back very straight.

The passage was empty. 'And now, dear heart, I am going to ask you to marry me, and if anyone interrupts me, I shall ignore them, and I hope you will do the same.'

Letitia was firmly tucked into his arms again. She looked at him, smiling.

'Yes, dear Jason, I'll do whatever you say.'

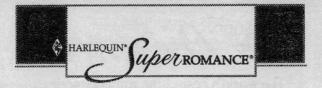

HARLEQUIN®
INTRIGUE

WE'LL LEAVE YOU BREATHLESS!

If you've been looking for thrilling tales of
contemporary passion and sensuous love stories
with taut, edge-of-the-seat suspense—then
you'll love Harlequin Intrigue!

Every month, you'll meet four new heroes
who are guaranteed to make your spine tingle
and your pulse pound. With them you'll enter
into the exciting world of Harlequin Intrigue—
where your life is on the line
and so is your heart!

THAT'S INTRIGUE—
ROMANTIC SUSPENSE
AT ITS BEST!

HARLEQUIN®
Makes any time special ®

INTDIR1

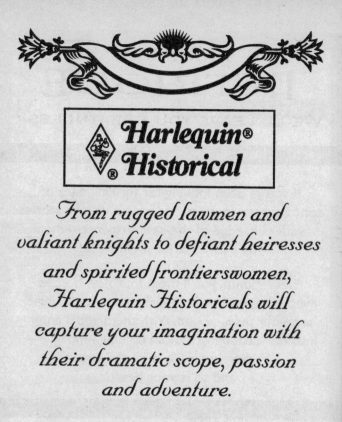

Harlequin® Historical

From rugged lawmen and valiant knights to defiant heiresses and spirited frontierswomen, Harlequin Historicals will capture your imagination with their dramatic scope, passion and adventure.

*Harlequin Historicals...
they're too good to miss!*

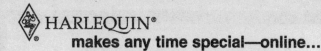

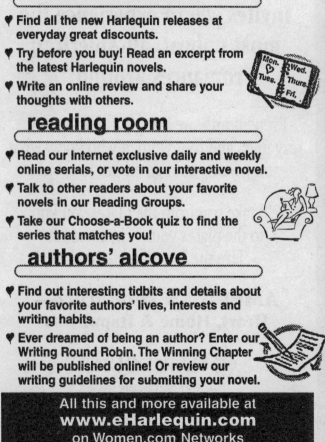